If Only

STORIES BY
Peter Stockland

If Only

STORIES BY
Peter Stockland

SIREN SONG

Typeset by Christopher Cargnello
Printed and bound in Canada
Printed by Marquis Book Printing Inc.

Dépôt legal – Bibliothèque et Archives nationales du Québec and the Library and Archives Canada, 2011

Library and Archives Canada Cataloguing in Publication

Stockland, Peter, 1955-
    If only / Peter Stockland.

Short stories.
ISBN 978-0-9783455-3-2

    I. Title.

PS8637.T617I3 2011   C813'.6   C2011-905906-1

Published by:
Siren Song Publishing
2331 Beaconsfield Avenue
Montréal, Québec H4A 2G9
www.sirensong.ca

Printed in Canada on 100% post-consumer recycled paper.

Acknowledgements

My gratitude goes to Siren Song publisher Zsolt Alapi for his fierce commitment to fiction writing. It made this collection possible. Thanks also to Christopher Cargnello for his design that brought everything together, and to the ever-diligent copy editor Cynthia Shannon for catching misplaced commas as if they were falling stars. I would like to acknowledge the help and sound advice given me by Bret Lott and members of the Image workshop at Mount Holyoke College. I was blessed with many great writing teachers over the years, including Frances Itani, who gave me the gift of detail, and David Helwig, who taught me fiction isn't journalism no matter how much journalism is fiction. Finally, I would like to thank all, anywhere, who ever shared a story with me, whether a long tale or a short burst of words. Listening is learning craft and dream.

Grateful acknowledgement to the following publications that first printed my writing: "Brothers" appeared in *Best Canadian Stories* (1989); "Greetings from Papineauville" in *Coming Attractions* (Oberon Press, 1990); "Cicerone" in *The Windsor Review* (1998); an excerpt from "Where the Lions Are" entitled "Red Hair Raphael" in *The Loose Canon #1* (2009); "Orange and Peel" in *Front & Centre #24* (2010); an excerpt from "The Family Accidental" appeared on the *Beat the Dust* website in printable chapbook form http://www.beatthedust.com/downloads/beatthedust/beat-the-dust-hidden-talent-apr11.pdf (2011)

For my family:
sine qua non

"*The horizon at which a human being arrives is like a grave stone: death is the origin and the stimulus for all searching.*"

MONSIGNOR LUIGI GIUSSANI
The Religious Sense

Contents

Introduction

Sometimes in the world of small publishing wonderful things can and do happen. For years you slug away at putting out books that mean something to you, worrying about the bills, the distribution, the readership—worrying about why you are doing all of this in the first place. And then you come upon a writer, someone whose words, passion, and insights reaffirm your faith in this most sullen of acts: putting feelings down into words that speak of meaningful coincidences, unexplained by cause and effect. For Jung, this was the "acausal connecting principle" —synchronicity— that linked mind to matter and affirmed the order in the universe, but I prefer to call it grace, for it is of such moments that good writing and writers are born.

It was through the most random and happiest of circumstances that I first met Peter Stockland, whose collection, *If Only*, you are about to read. Peter is an editor and journalist of some repute who had read a collection of stories I edited, received through an acquaintance. We met and we spoke about writing and about the writers we both loved: Raymond Carver, Faulkner, Chekhov, and many others. We became fast friends, and before long our conversation turned to Peter's own creative efforts. He showed me a longer story, "Where the Lions Are," and I was immediately struck by the power of his prose and the poignant immediacy of his characters who remained in my thoughts long after I had finished the last page. I was excited and energized, wanting to see more, so it came about inevitably and quite naturally as Peter showed me more of his stories that we conceived of this collection.

You have here a collection of stories that span time, the Canadian continent, as well as the vastest array of human experiences. The world of Stockland's characters is a dangerous and disconcerting one from a bloody standoff in BC, to the crisis of faith a priest undergoes after the loss of a relative, to lovers meeting secretly in abandoned motels while resurrecting their past, and to people living on the edge but trying to validate their lives through both random and meaningful acts. At the core of these stories lies the notion of regret and lost opportunities, treated with elegance and compassion by a writer whose fine ear for the rhythms of speech authenticates his characters and makes us feel with them through their trials, ecstasies, and grimmest moments. His are stories where coincidences are rendered to underscore our tenuous connectedness.

Perhaps the sum of this collection lies in the title story wherein the protagonist reflects on a missed opportunity with his friend's wife to whom he is attracted as he observes her "watching from the past where possibilities, chosen or unfulfilled, are like bright graveyard flowers that ceaselessly bloom and close, bloom and close." It is in this way that people, according to Peter Stockland, live their lives: living and dying to moments and promises unfulfilled, to desires acted upon or unrealized, to connections made or lost, to hopes destroyed and to memories that are as hauntingly real as lives lived with a purpose.

Peter Stockland is a writer of courage, conviction, and wisdom who dares to explore the vagaries of the heart. *If Only* is a testament in the profoundest sense of the word, where the writer is the witness to how we suffer in our mortality while pursuing the chance to be human.

ZSOLT ALAPI, September 2011

If Only

Brothers

We aren't killed yet, but our tongues are swelling and turning black from thirst. Allan's head lolls like when you pin a calf to the ground by the neck with your knee to slit its throat. Charlie's shoulders shake the way Ussher's did when I knelt on his chest. Archie and me are more all right. We clawed open a chink in a wall, scraped snow onto our fingers, pulled our hands back inside before their bullets hit. That was this morning. Or yesterday. I think yesterday. Or maybe not. My leg's still numb and I don't think it's bleeding.

I shouldn't have sent that note out. Not with those words on it. Archie knows. Even if he can't read, he knows. How does he know? How could he know? I don't know. But he does. I have to listen for it. For the click. That will mean he's getting ready. He could kill me. He could. Shoot me before they come in to get us. He could. He's like that. Crazier, in his way, than Allan. Way crazier. I shouldn't have sent that note out saying what it did. No matter how much we mean to each other, Archie could kill me. Shoot me for real. Say afterward he didn't mean it.

They've got a fire burning outside. Our tongues taste the smoke that seeps in through different wall cracks every time the wind shifts. When I crawled to the front of the cabin to fire at them that time, I could see the orange flames behind the screen of lodgepole pines. They're going to hang us. They'll take us to New Westminster for that. Not Kamloops. Kamloops first. The trial. Then New

3

Westminster. Their fire looked so warm.

We smell their food cooking. We hear more horses, more ranchers, more wagons arrive. I hear all the wagons leave again. Except the last one. That must mean they're getting ready. Keeping the wagon to take us back to Kamloops. Or our bodies. Kamloops first. Then New Westminster. I've never been to New Westminster in my life.

Why did I send that note out? Didn't I think Archie would know? What did I do it for? Why? Why did I send it out, saying what it did? I shouldn't have. Archie could kill me. For that he could.

Archie's a McLean and McLeans are killers. Isn't that what my father says? He says the McLeans are killers, father and sons. Hector's not, though. Hector's a McLean, but he's not a killer. Hector said no, I'm not going. You go. I'm not. Hector's strong. Stronger than Allan. Way stronger, even if younger. Allan's 25. Hector's eighteen. Or twenty. Remember that time he beat Allan up? Beat him senseless. Left those swollen black-and-yellow bruises on Allan's cheeks. Under his eyes.

Remember how afterward they kissed each other? On the lips. The way Archie and me thought only we did in secret. But Hector and Allan are brothers. I'm not a brother. I'm a Hare, not a McLean. Even though I killed Ussher. Even though it was me cutting his throat that killed him. Me kneeling on his chest in that clearing and cutting his throat that killed him. I'll always be a Hare. Never a McLean. Never.

Hector said you go, I'm not. I should have listened. I should have said, no, I'm not going either. Remember how Hector laughed in Allan's face at the talk about Sellah-Keetsa. Laughed. In his face. Isn't that what the fight was about? I think it was. I think so. I shouldn't have believed Allan about Sellah-Keetsa. Sellah-Keetsa's not coming. He never was. Never. Why did I believe Allan? Why do I love Archie? Oh, God, why do I love him so much?

I want to stand right beside Archie when they hang us. Maybe I'll reach out and touch his hand before the trap door opens. Who'll go first? Allan. I hope Allan. I hope Archie and I are left until last. Allan first because he led us here. It's his fault, really, even though it was me who killed Ussher. Charlie next for killing that white rancher. For target practice. Why'd you do that Charlie? Because you're a McLean, that's why. Charlie next. And then who? Me? Or Archie? Who first between him and me? I'm not a brother. Is that how they'll decide?

Unless Archie kills me first. He must have bullets left in his rifle. He could get mad enough thinking about that note. He's like that. Could I say I was sorry? Could I say I don't know why I sent it out? Could I lie and say it didn't say what he thinks it said? He can't read. He doesn't know for sure what it said. I could say no, Archie, you've got it all wrong. It didn't say that at all. But what if one of the white ranchers, when they do finally come in to get us, says where's Hare? Which one of you's Alex Hare? What do you mean the McLeans wouldn't let you surrender? What do you mean they forced you to come along? That's what they'll think the words on my note meant. Even if they don't believe them. One of them will say it out loud. Will Archie try to kill me then?

I want to stand beside Archie when they hang us. I want the rope to be long enough, loose enough, so I can lean over and kiss his lips. The way Hector kissed Allan. How will they put me in the wagon? How many of them will it take to lift me off this floor? They won't make me stand will they? Walk? They'll see my leg's broken. It is broken. I know the bone's sticking through the skin. I can't feel it, but I could tell the way Charlie pulled back and the way his breath came out and the way there was blood on his fingers after he touched my leg that the bone had come through.

I seen horses like that. When bones stick through a horse's leg it makes you think of a knife with half the blade busted off. All jagged that way. After you shoot them, they always stand and look at you for a minute. Like you could have done something else for them if you'd really wanted to. Like you've betrayed them just for the sake of it. Then they fall over onto their sides. Where's Charlie now? Over by the wall. Shoulders still shaking? Yes, though not so much. Where's Archie? I can't see him through all this smoke. Where's Hector? Wouldn't come. Said no. Beat Allan senseless. Allan's tongue is still lolling, thick and black. Where's Hector? Where's Hector now?

The white ranchers will say what do you mean the McLeans wouldn't let you surrender? What do you mean they forced you along? At some point one of them will say it. Maybe not when they first come in. Just before they hang us? No. Before then. In the wagon back to Kamloops? At the trial? I think at the trial. They'll ask. They'll think that's what my words meant. When they hear what I wrote, that's what the brothers will think, too. Maybe Allan won't care by then. Maybe Charlie will wish he hadn't tried to comfort me after he touched my leg where the bone came through. Tried to comfort me after he pulled back, the blood dripping off his fingers where he cut them open on me. What will Hector do? I know Archie suspects. I already know that.

Could I say it was the smoke that made me say what they'll think my note said? Could I say if they hadn't snuck up and tried to burn down the cabin over our heads in the middle of the night, and hadn't made so much thick smoke it almost choked us to death, maybe I wouldn't have lost my mind and written those words? Or could I say it was the pain? Jesus, oh, Jesus my leg hurt at first. Remember how it hurt? It was when I was running through the dark to get to the front of the cabin to fire at them.

I'd been sleeping. Dreaming. Then running. And the floor was giving way under my leg. Heard the crack and thought it was the floor giving way and my leg was caught in an animal trap someone had left under the old wood. Then powder stink in the dark and Charlie comforting me and saying you're shot, Alex, shot. And me thinking it was them coming in from outside. Coming to get us finally. Thinking will they kill us all right here or take us back? Kill or take?

Kill or take? And Charlie saying it was Archie, Alex. Archie shot you. He went crazy for a bit. He's all right now though. He didn't mean to shoot you. Where'd it hit? Here? In the leg? Here? Archie's all right now. Here? And drawing back and his breath drawing in quick and then hard out. Ssssttt. Phwow. The exact sound.

The pain made everything go silver. Then red. Black red. Black red as the blood when it came out of Ussher's throat. Black red as the blood on my chin when I stood in that clearing and licked the blood from his throat off the blade of my knife. Remember how that tasted, the blood from Ussher's throat and the blood from where licking my knife slit my tongue? Remember it mixing on my tongue? Is that what Hector tasted when he kissed Allan that time? Is it? Is it? Oh, God, I love Archie. I want to kiss him so they all see.

Maybe I could say it was everything going silver and red and red and silver and silver and silver and red and silver silver silver silver red that made me write those words. Made me write words I didn't mean in a way that will make those men outside believe something I didn't mean to say. Would they believe that, the brothers? Would Archie? Even if I had lied to him once already?

They are going to hang us. There's no Sellah-Keetsa coming. Did Allan really believe he would come? I believed it. Didn't I? I had to have, otherwise I would have done what Hector did. I would have said no. I would have said, Archie, don't go either. He's younger than I am. Two years. He's only fifteen. He would have listened to me. Wouldn't he have? Even if he is a McLean. Even if his mother was Indian and I'm a Hare and never will be a McLean. Never. Never. Even though I killed Ussher. With my knife. And tasted his blood, too. Salt.

There's no Sellah-Keetsa coming. There's not going to be an uprising. There's not going to be any old Nicole chief bringing his people up the Valley to attack the white ranchers outside waiting for us. There's not going to be any chance for us to ride out of here, shooting at the white ranchers, ride across the border, get away and

7

go south. Far south, like Allan says. I know that. Archie knows that. Charlie? Maybe. Allan? No. If Allan could talk, he'd still say no, we can't surrender. Don't surrender. Wait. For Sellah-Keetsa. Who's not coming. Who will never come. That was just Allan dreaming. That was just Allan afraid.

Remember the first time Archie touched me? Or I touched him. Which was it? It matters to remember, but I can't. I can't remember who touched whom first. It's as if it hasn't happened yet. Like where we'll stand when they hang us. But it did. There was a first time. And it was after that Allan got afraid. It was after he killed Schubert in that fight, wasn't it? After he killed Schubert in that fight over the lie Archie told. The lie Archie told about Schubert calling him a half-breed and spitting on him and hitting him with a stick for speaking Shuswap to Mrs. Schubert in Mara's store.

It was when we were coming back from dumping Schubert's body in that alkali lake I knew about. Charlie had said dump it in the river, but I said no. I know a lake up in the hills where no one goes. Ever. We could take it there. No one will find out. That's exactly what I said, isn't it? No one will find out. We were riding back. There was that white winter moon. Remember the way Schubert's body hissed as it slid through the dead-white bunch grass on the way through the hills to the lake? Remember the way the rope tied taut to his body glistened like spun ice stretching back from Archie's horse? And forcing the horses out across the shore ice into the deeper water? Then he was gone. Sinking. Sinking. Lying on the bottom. We couldn't tell if it was his eyes we were looking at or stones.

And it was when we were coming back that Archie admitted his lie, wasn't it? The two of us had fallen back. We were riding side by side and Allan was leading, a quarter-mile ahead. Then Charlie. Then us. And Archie saying no, it wasn't calling him half-breed or spitting on him or hitting him with a stick or speaking Shuswap. It was shaking him by the shoulders for sticking his hand up Mrs. Schubert's dress as she was bending over putting jars into a box at the counter of Mara's store. You better tell Allan. My exact words. You better tell Allan you lied, Archie. Or I will. Or I will. My exact threat. Who touched whom? First.

It doesn't matter. That was Allan. Allan who had taken his knife and cut one of Schubert's eyes out and carved the eyeball out of the skull socket and pinched the pulp between his fingers and thrown it to the raven that hunched like an old Chinaman on the edge of that square of white earth down by the China shacks just up from the river. Hunched like it had bet on the fight, and had bet right and was waiting for its winnings. And Schubert not quite yet dead. Still breathing. Twisting. Moaning. And when the knife went into his eye, recoiling so hard upward he might have been getting back up on his feet to fight some more. And the marks on his throat starting to shine dull red where Allan had crushed his windpipe. Bare hands crushing a man's windpipe. And that raven. Picking up that eye in its beak. Its black wings flapping. Thut-thuwa. Thut-thuwa. Perching on the high branch of that lodgepole pine. Eating its reward. And then Archie's lie. And Schubert's body under black water. And Allan saying it doesn't matter. Doesn't matter. Only a white rancher. And my father a white rancher. And Kamloops full of white ranchers. Doesn't matter. That was Allan afraid. Sellah-Keetsa came afterward. That was Allan dreaming.

And then Ussher and the white ranchers coming after us. Threatening to arrest us. For Schubert? For killing Schubert? No. For Charlie stealing a horse. For Charlie listening to Allan and going and stealing Palmer's black mare. And for Charlie listening to Allan and riding the mare through where he knew he'd be seen. Listening to Allan and actually getting off Palmer's black mare outside Mara's store and taking time to tie its reins, and going into Mara's store and buying a new knife. Taking his time looking them over. Saying my old one's busted. The blade snapped when I was sharpening it. Sharpening it to slit a calf's throat ha-ha. And testing the blade against his thumb when he came out to the small crowd gathered around Palmer's mare. And Ussher in the clearing when they caught up to us saying just give back the horse. Just give it back. Or I'll have to arrest you. Allan? Charlie? Knowing us all by name, but leaving Archie and me out on purpose, as if we hadn't become involved just yet and he wanted us not to for our sakes. That was Allan gone crazy. Even after Hector beat him senseless. That was Allan knowing all along we'd end up in this cabin. Leading us here all along. Waiting for Sellah-Keetsa. I never dreamed killing Ussher would be so easy. Him doubling over like that and me on the ground, already off my horse before Ussher fell forward and the powder still thick black smoke from Allan's rifle and the other white ranchers cowering like sullen cows near that lodgepole, their faces saying don't shoot us now Allan please now don't do something crazy and shoot us too we're just here to help we just came along he's all right you shot him but he's all right and we'll just get him back to Kamloops and we'll fix him up and you keep the horse. Even Palmer's face, saying you keep my mare, Allan, you keep it. Or let Charlie have it. Whatever you boys decide between yourselves. And no one saying a word with Charlie's rifle and Allan's rifle pointed at them. Their faces just saying everything and me running before I even hit the ground across that wordless clearing. And how easy that knife cut through Ussher's throat once I knelt on his chest. And taking his coat off his heaving shoulders and watching the blood just spuming into the snow. And the salt of his blood and mine. And Charlie shooting that white rancher who said coward. Just for target practice. Why'd that rancher have to say that? Coward. Spitting it. Falling over backwards clutching his stomach. And me. Licking the knife. That salt. Giving Ussher's coat to Archie. Draping it over Archie's shoulders like I'd just bought my best girl a present from Mara's store.

It was Archie I was dreaming about when I woke up and started running toward the front of the cabin. I was dreaming we were running in summer-dust light down a narrow trail through shoulder-high bunch grass into a stand of lodgepole, where we came out riding bent against our horses' necks. Smelling their red-brown sweat. Breaking clear into a meadow, chasing a blood-brown and white calf across a wide plain toward the river curling in currents white as the lariat Archie looped over the calf's head, neck, throat. And then I was dropping onto it, pinning it to the ground by the neck with my knee, pulling out my knife to slit its throat and looking down at Ussher's body jerking underneath me, spilling blood like salt-coloured seed from its stomach and throat except that it was Archie not Ussher I was on top of and his lips were twisting the words killer coward killer coward killer coward like knife points into my eyes and we were struggling and rolling and clawing and rolling through clay dust toward the edge of the river. Then I was up. Running. Running away from Archie. Then awake. Running toward him and thinking the floor had given way under me.

It was Archie who shot me. It was Archie who made me write that note. Told me to write it. I should have just written what he said to write. What he said Allan wanted. Allan moaning. Tongue lolling. It was after the ranchers tried to burn the cabin down over our heads and couldn't because the hay they used was too wet. Archie saying Allan says for you to write on a piece of paper that we'll never surrender. Allan not even able to talk. Archie saying Allan says to write we'll never surrender. Never. The sleeve of the coat I put over Archie's shoulder coming toward me through all the smoke. His hand stretched out of the sleeve. Ussher's coat. His hand opening and showing the small piece of white paper. The lump of charcoal. Archie rolling me over onto my side under all the smoke. Rolling me over like he was going to come into me from behind the way he likes to when we're together in secret. Putting the charcoal on top of the paper. Saying write the note, Alex. His exact words. Did he know what I would write instead? Did he think my lie would make up for his?

I should have written just what he said to write. Not what he must have known I'd write. Not what I wrote. I should have just written the McLean brothers say they will never surrender and that you can kill them a thousand times over but they will have revenge against those who lie against them in God's name. I wrote that. I did write it. But then I wrote underneath I wish to know what you all have against me. If you have anything, please let me know what it is. Alex J. Hare. December 1879. I shouldn't have written that. I didn't mean what they'll take it to mean. I didn't mean it that way. Didn't.

Did I even mean to kill Ussher? I never would have believed it could be so easy. I could tell them I only wanted his coat to give to Archie. I could say that. If Archie doesn't kill me first. If he doesn't find out what I wrote. What I wrote will matter. It will matter. Wait. Listen. There. The click. The click. The bullet. Dropping. From inside? Archie? From outside? Where's Archie? The smoke. Are they coming? I'm not a McLean. Archie? Archie? Archie? Archie, where are you? Charlie? Charlie. Charlie. Listen. Listen. Who is it? Archie? There. The click. Archie? Charlie? McLeans are killers. Archie. Archie where are you? Sellah-Keetsa's not coming. Allan can't talk. Hector said no. Archie. They're going to hang us. I love Archie. I'm not a brother. I love Archie. Oh God I loved that taste of salt on my tongue.

Greetings From Papineauville

It is already Sunday evening. The middle of May. Still quite warm. And quiet. Peaceful.

Elsewhere in Quebec, politics is in the air again. Language. Sovereignty. It is 1989, not 1980, but in Ottawa, in la Ville de Québec, something is rising as if this were the referendum year all over again. The people who promise change by saying the same things over and over are waving their arms, stirring the breeze.

But that's outside. In Papineauville, Achille and Coco walk up rue de l'Église together as always. They climb the small hill from the river. Both of them hold fishing rods in their left hands. In his right hand, Achille holds a grey cord with a large silver hook on it. The hook pierces the gills of three fish. The fish turn speckled brown bodies in slow revolutions.

The street divides around the patch of grass and the blue reflecting pond that is parc Saint-Sauveur. Achille unhooks the largest fish. Coco hooks a finger through the gill. The fish trails him home, its tail skating above the dust.

Achille walks another block until he reaches rue des Patriotes, the main street of Papineauville. Its west end leads to Ottawa. Its east end leads to Montreal. He turns back. In a single motion he waves good night to Coco and tosses his cigarette away. It glows behind him. Smoke floats from it after he is gone.

"Christ de merde," Jules says. "Maudite bande d'anglais sales chien de bâtard."

He hangs upside down on a Jungle Gym in the playground of l'École Louis-Joseph Papineau. As he speaks, his T-shirt descends like an upside-down curtain over his face. Christiane waits until the red cotton covers his eyes, then slaps him on the bare stomach. Her fingers leave a red mark almost the colour of his shirt.

"Tais-toi," she says. "Arrêtes de blasphèmer. Tu me casses les oreilles, toi."

She slaps Jules again, catching cotton this time as he swings up to avoid her. He drops to the ground upright, grabbing her left hand at the wrist. He pulls her toward him and tries to hold her and avoid being hit at the same time. He kisses her, laughing. She breaks free and stands outside the circle of the apparatus, laughing.

He sings:

Les maudits anglais tête-carrées,
Baptême, baptême.
Les maudits anglais tête-carrées,
Baptême, baptême
Les maudits anglais tête-carrées,
Je souhaite pouvoir les tuer
Les maudits anglais shit de tête-carrées.

He laughs as loudly as he's sung. His voice carries over the lawn and across rue des Patriotes. A woman in white running shoes has one hand on the door of Dépanneur Turgeon when she turns toward the sound. Christiane runs across the grass, covering her ears. Jules follows her, his voice bounding ahead of them both.

Ghislaine slits the white fish belly and spreads the flaps. She hooks two fingers into the cavity. Bright burgundy guts trail the fingers back out. They soak into the copy of *Le Droit* she's spread across the table. The newspaper ink mixes with the blood on her fingers,

14

blackening the red. She cuts the head and tail off the fish, then carries them out to the back porch. In the last of the evening light, she drops them into the cat's bowl.

Achille calls from the hallway. He's going to the dépanneur to get some cigarettes for the morning.

Coco guts and washes his fish quickly and wraps the refuse neatly. He walks outside and stuffs the bundle in the garbage can, tamping the lid down to keep out the raccoons and cats. The metal grunts and grinds. Through the kitchen window, he hears the television coming from the living room. He goes inside and sees his wife asleep again on the sofa. He gently pushes her lower jaw up to close her mouth. She rouses at his touch. She falls back to sleep.

Two men get out of the green Chrysler that has pulled up on rue des Patriotes across from a white frame building. The sign has been taken off the building, but the outline of the letters still identifies it as Garage Félix. One window has a crescent-moon hole in the lower right corner. Behind the glass a red and black sign says À VENDRE.

The man in the navy suit who was driving the Chrysler stands in the middle of the street waiting for a blue Chev half-ton to pass. His companion, also wearing a navy suit, catches up to him. At the door of Garage Félix, the larger man stands back and lets his smaller companion enter first.

Ghislaine stretches the Saran Wrap tightly over the white plate on which the fish lies. Water turns soap to bubbles on her hands beneath the tap. Achille comes up the walk as she settles into a chair on the front gallery. When she raises the match to the tip of the cigarette he gives her, she can still smell river water, weeds, fish blood on her skin. He slumps in the chair beside her. The twin red tips of their cigarettes mark them. They talk quietly about having the fish for supper tomorrow night.

"Bourassa vendu," Jules says. "Christ de merde vendu."
He sits on the wall in front of l'École Louis-Joseph Papineau,

drumming the heels of his Converse high-tops against the concrete. Christiane sits beside him. The zipper of her quilted ski jacket is done up to her chin.

"Arrête-moi-donc," she says. "Parles pas de politiques. Je n'ai rien à faire avec la politique. C'est ben plate."

Jules's friend Roger stands with his back turned to them. He watches a man tie a spaniel to the post outside Garage Félix. A woman in a white sweater takes the man's arm and they enter together.

Roger drains a can of orange juice into his mouth. The aluminum clanks hitting the sidewalk. It's the sound the empty beer cans made hitting the wall behind the arena last winter when Roger got drunk before the game against Hawkesbury. The juice can grinds and snaps when he crushes it with his foot. He turns to Christiane.

"Indépendance," he says. "Québec libre."

He smiles at Jules. Light and cigarette smoke drift out of Garage Félix when a man in a red-and-black plaid jacket opens the door and steps inside.

Coco clicks a leash onto the silver loop of his dog's leather collar and tugs. The dog rises slowly, shakes so that leash and loop jingle like Noël bells. He snorts. Snuffles. Walks up to the corner beside his master in a bedroom-slipper shuffle. His head is bent at a sharp angle to the grass. His eyes blink sleepily.

The larger man in the navy suit is marking numbers in an itinerary book. The smaller man is trying to find someone who'll take charge of turning off the television when the premier arrives at Garage Félix for his speech. A tight circle is watching the set at the far end of the room. They butt cigarettes nervously into crushed styrofoam cups. The Quebec Liberal party has rented Garage Félix for the by-election. Four volunteers spent Saturday converting the abandoned shop into headquarters for their local candidate. Laying clean plywood on the floor. Setting up tables. Putting up an equal number of posters showing the candidate and the premier. Finding a place for the coffee urn.

Buying styrofoam cups. But the Canadiens trail 3-1.

Steam rises from the spout of the coffee pot and curls around Ghislaine's face. She pours milk into Achille's cup. Only half a teaspoon of sugar. His blood pressure. He taps her lightly on the bum when she puts his coffee down. The premier's face looks up at her. It lies flat on her kitchen table. A small image of a smiling man in glasses surrounded by typewritten words on the front page of *Le Droit*.

"Il sera ici ce soir, hein?" Achilles says. "Monsieur le premier ministre."

The page rattles when he turns it. His coffee slurps when he drinks it.

Coco sees the kids leaning against the low wall in front of the school. He waves, but they don't see him.

Looking down the block, he sees a knot of people standing outside Garage Félix. There's a car he doesn't recognize parked on the other side of the street. He goes into the dépanneur and buys milk for the morning. Cheese for his sandwiches. Cigarettes. Four Molsons to help him sleep.

"Qu'est-ce qui se passe là-bas?" Coco asks. "Pourquoi il y a du monde devant l'ancien garage?"

The woman behind the counter stops a finger in mid-air above the cash register.

"On a d'la grande visite," she says. "Le premier ministre. Monsieur Bourassa."

Coco sniffs. He shifts the brown grocery bag to the crook of his left arm. The woman's finger punches the keys.

"Bourassa," he says. "Innocent."

He holds out his right hand for his change.

Christiane watches Coco bend at the bicycle rack outside the dépanneur and untie the dog's leash. She sees him slowly straighten and start home. The little dog pads at his master's side as if he'd rather be sleeping on his front paws than walking on them. She turns on

Jules, on Roger. Tells them they're idiots. That they talk nonsense.

"Niaiseux," she says. "Vous avez des têtes à Papineau, vous autres. Indépendance. Québec libre. Les vraies têtes à Papineau."

"Ben oui," Jules says. "Ma grand-mère était une Papineau. Son nom de famille était Papineau. Je pense pas que c'est la même famille, mais quand même. Ouais, j'ai une tête de Papineau. C'est une bonne tête. Pas comme toi, Christiane Cauchon, grosse tête de cochon."

Roger laughs loudly at the pun. At Jules having the nerve to insult a girl. The two boys light cigarettes. The smoke Jules exhales clings in Christiane's hair. She waves a hand in front of her face to clear it and coughs theatrically. It leaves his taste in her mouth.

Ghislaine puts the fish on a lower rack in the fridge and makes room for the milk. She sees an ad in *Le Droit* for fresh spinach on special at the Provigo in Thurso. She says she'll get some tomorrow to go with the fresh fish. Achille says he can pick it up on his way home from the mill. He says put a note in his lunch kit, otherwise he'll forget. He slips an arm around her waist. Smacks his lips.

"Des bons épinards avec une bonne truite," Achille says. "Hein, ça serait bon, ma femme."

The small man in the navy suit stands beside the TV set, sipping coffee. He says the premier will be inside in about five minutes – he's just outside meeting people and shaking hands. The large man in the navy suit looks between the smoke that hangs from the roof and the heads of the people sitting at the paper-covered tables. He signals his companion. Larry Robinson lets a shot go from the Bruins' blue line. 3-3.

Jules holds Christiane's right arm tightly as she pulls away. Her arm comes out of the ski jacket's black sleeve and he's left holding the empty quilted cotton. He tries to catch her by the left wrist, but she moves back too quickly and he tumbles clumsily from the wall. She warns him she'll leave if he goes with Roger.

She's not laughing now.

"C'est pas drôle," she says.

Roger kicks the empty juice can. It skitters and clacks down the sidewalk. When it stops, it turns slowly once on its axis.

"Viens, ti-Papineau," he says. "On s'en va."

He wants to cross rue des Patriotes to Garage Félix and yell something. He wants to get up close to Bourassa's face and holler something that will make the people near the premier give chase. He wants to run. Run like hell down the street. Jump over hedges in front yards. Duck around the corners of the houses.

"On va lui donner un bon 'greeting' de Papineauville," Roger says. "Comme les Patriotes de quarante-sept."

Jules looks at Christiane. She is already half-turned away from him. He looks at Roger, then across rue des Patriotes. The window light spilling from Garage Félix mixes with the harsh conical floods of two television cameras. In the shadows between the two lights, the premier's arm comes up, reaches out into the darkness for another hand to touch.

"Quarante-sept?" Jules says. "Trente-sept. C'était en trente-sept, les Patriotes."

His grandmother gave him a book once called *Les Patriotes de Trente-Sept*. He remembers reading how Papineau urged his rebels to rise for La Petite Nation – the name of Papineau's seigneurie, the name of his dream. He remembers reading how the English slaughtered Papineau's Patriotes in the bitter winter of 1837. How they hanged the others after the rebellion failed.

Roger waves his hand impatiently.

"Un détail," he says.

Christiane turns her back.

The large man in the navy suit reaches across the head of the man closest to the set and turns off the game.

"Les Canadiens vont gagner," he says with the hearty certainty of a man who works for a majority government.

Jules remembers his grandmother's finger pointing. It was the flesh of her hand, in the Sunday evening light, that made him realize for the first time how old she was. He was fishing with his father from a small bridge over rivière Petite-Nation. They'd all gone to Huberdeau to buy early summer corn and stopped to fish on the way back.

His grandmother got out of the station wagon and crossed the bridge just as a fish struck Jules's line. Kneeling to free the hook, he saw the hem of her pale-grey and coral dress above her thick brown stockings. Turning, he saw the creases in the leather of her bitter-smelling black shoes. He was looking up, pinning the wet, flexing fish to the ground with one hand, when she pointed.

"Ça – ça c'est nous autres," she said.

The fish flipped free and Jules scrambled to grab its slick flesh. His grandmother was back in the station wagon when he looked up again. She sat beside his mother in the rear seat, turning stiffly to look out the window once or twice.

He and his father teased her for a bit, asking her what she'd meant. Asking her what they were? Birds? Hydro poles? When she wouldn't answer, they stopped teasing. They were silent down all the long hills home. Fields and trees, sometimes water, streamed past.

Coco sets the empty beer bottles in the cupboard case on the back porch. He leaves the outside light on for Roger. He leaves it on, too, for his eldest son, Michel. He leaves an upstairs hall light on for his wife. It frightens him when she tries to find her way upstairs to bed in the dark.

The small man, the large man, stand side by side under the cigarette smoke, smoking cigarettes of their own, glancing at their watches. Sweat trickles down one's short, dark neck, sticks under the armpits of the other. They were supposed to be in Saint-André-Avellin at 7:30 – two hours ago. One says at least they won't have to compete with the hockey game now. It'll be long over before they arrive. The other says unless there's overtime. They both nod. Les maudits playoffs. Always bad news for spring by-elections.

Jules's grandmother sat on the back stoop. Woodsmoke drifted toward her from a small fire his father had started to cook the corn. There was a large silver pot of water beside her. The pot had a hooped handle. The handle hung from a hook attached to an iron rod arched over the fire.

He was crossing the yard to put out the fishing rods and tackle in the shed when he heard her tearing open the corn. The backs of her pale hands were ridged, the texture of the tough green leaves she parted. She ran her fingers over the conical cob, cleaning away the white-yellow filaments stuck to the knuckle-shaped kernels. She sang softly, under her breath, a children's song about water.

She might have been singing to the corncobs she pulled from the burlap sack. When she spoke, it was absently, as if to the light.

"La rivière," she said.

Jules stood in the drifting smoke. His eyes and throat stung with dryness.

"Grandmama?" he said.

She might have been dead the way she didn't answer. She was dead when he understood what she meant. When he understood it was the water she'd pointed at from the bridge. In her eyes they were the river. All of it: water, fish, name. La Petite Nation. Papineau's greeting. Papineau's dream.

Coco bunches his pillow under his head. Lies on his left side. Then his right. Back and forth. Lies on his back. Gets up and pees the Molsons. From his bedroom window he can look down rue de l'Église and see the unlit space that's the river.

Roger will go soon. Michel already lives in Western Canada. Somewhere called Tsawassen. Everyone in Papineauville laughed, at first, trying to pronounce the name of the town where Coco's eldest boy lived. Tsawassen. Now, Christmas cards arrive signed: Seasons Greetings/Joyeux Noël – Mike and Cynthia, Tania and Jason.

21

Roger looks across the street. The premier is going inside. He's making his way forward in the darkness through a small circle of supporters backlit in the doorway.

"Vas-y, Jules," Roger says. "On peut dire en anglais: 'Greetings from Papineauville, Mr. Bourassa.' Quand il se tournera, comme un chien sale anglais vendu, on peut y dire en pleine face: 'Va chier maudit anglais vendu, Bourassa, les Patriotes de Papineauville t'haïssent.' Ça va être l'fun, eh, ti-Papineau?"

Christiane turns back.

"Je m'en vais," she says. "C'est pas drôle."

She squints at the crowd. Names some of the people. Asks Jules if he thinks they'll just let him insult the premier. If he thinks they'll just stand with their hands in their pockets while he runs away laughing.

She turns away. Takes a step. Another. The quilted pattern of her jacket will disappear if she takes a third. If Jules lets her go, the next time he sees her she won't see him. He calls to her to stop.

His ankle hurts from his tumble off the wall. He felt something grind inside when he fell. He doesn't know how fast he could run anyway. He takes two hobbling steps. Turns to Roger.

"Juste cries fort d'ici, Roger," he says. "Ça serait mieux."

Roger has the loudest lungs and strongest throat in Papineauville. When he came in the arena drunk last winter and cheered for Hawkesbury, people in the seats around him covered their ears as if a car horn were stuck. But Roger has already stepped off the curb. His left foot already rests on rue des Patriotes.

Christiane takes another step. Turns to look over her shoulder.

"Vas imiter ton petit chum, Jules," she says.

He takes a step toward her. Looks again at Roger. A drift of woodsmoke comes from somewhere down the street.

The premier himself enters Garage Félix. Supporters mill, begin to applaud. He moves inside, in a cone of television lights, beaming.

Ghislaine writes the reminder on a yellow Post-it Note before she goes to bed: EPINARDS. OUBLIES PAS. She tucks it in the fold of the wax paper covering Achille's sandwich. She puts an apple in and sets the lunch box on the back-porch shelf. The cat jumps off a green-cushioned chair and trots toward his bowl. When he sees Ghislaine is empty-handed, he stops and looks appalled at her treachery.

She turns out the lights, checks to make sure the back door is unlocked for Jules. He'll catch hell in the morning for staying out late on a school night. But she isn't going to lock him out.

Her nightdress is cool against her breasts. She shivers, sliding into bed. She curls against Achille. Achille rolls onto his back. Even asleep, he feels the safety of Ghislaine beside him. He lets his breath out slowly, like floating up for air.

Cicerone

Father Bernard touched the wall with his outstretched arm, signalling the last lap of the day. He lolled, briefly, in the bright water at the shallow end of the pool. Only his nose and the crown of his head were visible to the handful of resort guests lounging on deck chairs.

Rising, his grey hair tufted, his torso thick and still strong, he might have been Bernini's Moor emerging from one of the minor fountains in the Piazza Navona. Then his white legs in their pale blue trunks emerged, and the effect was lost.

"*Gelato*," he said. "Do you know what that means?"

His nephew, Gavin, put down his sketch pad and pencil, reached beneath the chaise longue, and brought out the phrase book with the line drawing of the Colosseum and the Dome of St. Peter's on the cover. He flipped the pages.

The priest balanced on one leg like a retired acrobat. He rubbed a clean white towel meticulously across his shoulders and back. He patted his chest and folded the towel into a neat, white square. The cocoa scent of tanning cream absorbed him.

"*Gelato*," he said, "is the Italian word for ice cream. It is the best ice cream in the world. When we go to Rome, we will buy you some. You will love it. Once you have eaten it, you will remember it like your own name."

Gavin smiled up as though a dish of the best ice cream in the world was being held at arm's length from him, as if he had its taste, cold and addictive, on his tongue. He closed the phrase book and balanced it on the arm of the chair.

"You bought mother ice cream once," he said. "Remember?"

His sarcasm kissed Father Bernard like rain. The tone mimicked Carmelia counterattacking during an argument. It meant she'd told Gavin the story. Father Bernard did not know what had prompted either the tone or the telling. He tilted his head to the left – his habitual gesture for demanding apology or at least explanation.

But the boy, as if he'd given away enough, turned to watch a man in red bikini bathing briefs bounce twice on the diving board. The recoil of the board reverberated and they watched his body rise, stall and become a jackknife silhouette.

"All things return to earth," the priest said as the man disappeared beneath his own splash.

It sounded like shopworn Scripture: tritely mysterious. Father Bernard had been born with a pedant's gift for moving things to higher, drier ground. He stood over Gavin and picked up the phrase book. Holding it open in both hands, he might have been back in his classroom signaling quiet before beginning the senior boys' Latin declension drill.

"No. I won't be quiet. Who asked who to come here? I should never have come here with you."

An elderly woman's voice bolted across the waist-high hedge and black iron fence that separated the pool from the rolling front lawn of the resort. She sat upright on the grass, her legs tucked under her, speaking to a man who lay on his back. He was dressed in a black suit and heavy black shoes, the kind immigrant men wore ashore early in the century. Sweat trickled from under his sideburns.

She was all in pink. Even her head was swathed in a crepe-de-Chine turban that came low on her forehead, framing a face Father Bernard could only think of as reptilian. The man reached out his hand to touch her arm, but she drew away and left his thick fingers fluttering. Though she lowered her voice, the movement of her mouth mimed the litany of an old quarrel.

Whom, Father Bernard thought, reflexively correcting her grammar. Who brought whom here? Who misunderstood whom to start the fight?

"I used to think you were so tall," Gavin said. "I thought you owned the church."

The priest turned back to his nephew, who was doodling a caricature of a diver jackknifed above the pool. The boy had talent, perhaps a vocation. The trip to Rome was to show him the treasures, to let him experience real art, while he was still young enough to benefit.

That was how Carmelia phrased it. Father Bernard agreed, though he had silent hopes for other influences as well. Gavin was baptized but had not even taken his first communion. There was no sign of preparation for him receiving the sacrament of confirmation.

That particular argument lay both behind them and before them. Now was not the time to raise it. Not when Carmelia was paying the shot for the trip to Rome. Not when her good graces were responsible for them spending the weekend at this American resort to plan their itinerary.

His sister was an architect in both her professional and personal lives. Churches were pure geometry to her. Faith was like the disappointments – the dangers – of gravity.

"Your mother," Father Bernard said, "loved *gelato. Caffe gelato*. Coffee ice cream. She wanted it for breakfast, lunch and supper."

He knew the danger of coming back to the subject after he'd escaped, but this time he couldn't resist. The story had already been told about him at least as far as its climax. He needed to have a say in its ending.

Gavin seemed to have lost interest. His fleeting look could

have been amusement or annoyance at the incongruity of his mother lapping up a minor luxury paid for by an uncle who always wore the same black suit. He became wholly absorbed by his sketch.

He gave the diver in the drawing huge, distended hands, more like angels' wings than anything human and inserted a hook through the waistband of the bathing suit. A rope extended from the hook to the top of the page, holding the figure in an absurd posture of momentary balance. "Return to earth," he wrote in large letters at the bottom of the page. Father Bernard did not need to see the caricature's face to recognize himself.

"I'm going," he said, "to change for lunch."

Pushing through the irongate and stepping onto the lawn, he looked down the slope to the beach where sunbathers were moving back from the flowing tide. He saw Carmelia wading into the sea, holding up the hem of her floral sundress against the swells. A man was close to her, and she seemed to be talking to him. She was deft at meeting strangers. Father Bernard thought she looked up at him. He waved to her, but she didn't respond. As he passed the woman in pink, her voice dropped to a bitter rustle.

The old man's hands were palm down in the waistband of the black trousers. His head had lapsed back onto the grass. His eyes were open and he gave the impression of staring at something high in the Mary-blue Maine sky.

The waitress could have been a lifeguard. She wore aubergine shorts the shape and texture of a man's swimming trunks and a loose cotton T-shirt that declared her the property of the Georgetown Hoyas. Her legs and arms, when she set down the soup, displayed muscles that would have been thought embarrassingly masculine at the time Father Bernard was ordained.

He had preached a homily once on the dangers of the daughters of Eve developing outward strength and neglecting inward grace.

A deputation from Women Affirming Shared Ministry complained to the diocesan office. The bishop, a bully who permitted brutal post-Vatican II attacks on altar rails and statuary, sent Father Bernard a curt note about inclusiveness. From the way Carmelia smiled when he railed to her about the influences of feminists running graduate schools of theology, he knew she was involved behind the scenes.

"My brother is going to be our guide in Rome," she said now. "He lived there for years. He speaks perfect Italian."

The cut went over the head of their youngish lunch guest, an American named either Ronald or Derik. It was not lost on Father Bernard. It was aimed directly at him, though why here, why now was a mystery.

The reference was to his long-ago fumble at a café in Rome. He had meant to say *prego* and said *gelato* instead. The gaffe should have produced one of those comic family stories retold to new acquaintances. Instead, through a grotesque accident of timing, his faux pas had become bound in memory to Carmelia's fright and anger at being mauled by a sweating Roman with bad teeth.

"Enjoy," the waitress said, setting the last bowl of soup in front of Gavin.

Father Bernard had to hastily guard his eyes as her T-shirt gaped when she bent forward, exposing the tops of her breasts. He looked past her and down the lawn. He expected to see the elderly couple still sitting below the hedge but they were gone, their absence like a hole cut in the centre of a painting. The beach, the sea, the sky were like pentimento through the missing square.

When he looked back to the table, he almost jumped at the sight of them standing in the doorway leading from the patio into the main dining room. They stood side by side without speaking until a tuxedoed maître d', a counterpoint of severe formality to the patio waitress, escorted them away.

Despite the hot sun, the sluice of the sea, the priest suddenly felt as if it might begin to snow. It would not have surprised him if large, fat flakes had begun drifting down into his soup. It was not just the day but his life that allowed such peculiarity. He lowered his head for the blessing. Carmelia fumbled in her purse and took a pair of sunglasses from a green leather case.

She had insisted on sitting on the patio so they could relax in the sun and enjoy the sea as they ate. Ronald – or Derik – was the man she had been talking to by the water's edge. Spaniel-coloured curls grew around his ears. Father Bernard was never to question his sister's taste in friends, American, Canadian or otherwise. He made the sign of the Cross and was pleasantly aware of Gavin's hand tracing an awkward mirror image in the air. There were pepper plants in terra cotta pots around the patio and their earthy pungency, mixed with the salt air, reminded him of the sharp warm smells of his student haunts down the hill from the Pontifical University of St. Thomas Aquinas.

He planned to take Gavin through the area when they were in Rome, working up from the birthday-cake gaudiness of the monument to Italy's sad last king, Victor Emmanuel, on the Piazza Venetia, retracing his steps to the Angelicum, pointing out all the things the tourists missed, stopping to eat *gelato* in the sun at an outdoor cafe. He would do it on the third or fourth day, right after the surprise he had in store for their visit to the Vatican.

There was power in such moments to sow the seeds of vocations or at least, in Gavin's case, commitment to the sacramental life. Carmelia insisted on leaving the pursuit of faith to the boy. She stubbornly resisted Father Bernard's argument that children cannot pursue anything unless they are first led to the point where it is visible, tangible, appreciable.

"Amen," he said, regretting the slight note of defiance.

His eyes met Carmelia's as he raised his head. She put on the sunglasses and became opaque. He was ordained the year she started high school. As a child, she had looked up to him naturally. In her mid-20s, near completion of her architecture degree, she inverted the hierarchy at will.

The weight of his education, erudition and priestly position worked against him, as if he were the victim of a perfected judo flip. Like so many women of her age, she had been left unattended at a critical time. She was allowed to decide things for herself too early and made the common, disastrous mistake of overvaluing individual power and technique.

"Not much time," she was saying to their guest. "Two days at most. Then Florence. We'd rather spend our time in Tuscany. Rome is just a huge, filthy traffic jam. Forty-eight hours and we're out."

Their guest nibbled the corner of his steak sandwich. It had arrived late and lay on his plate like puddled oil. He did not seem to care. His focus was Carmelia. Unable to remember his name, Father Bernard mentally dubbed him The Huntsman though it was not all that clear who was pursuing whom.

"See what you have to and get out, right?" The Huntsman laughed. "That's what I do, too."

"Seen one chiesa of the BVM, you've seen them all," Carmelia laughed, too.

The Huntsman paused in mid-chew.

"BVM?"

He worked the acronym against its possibilities.

"Blessed Virgin Mary," Carmelia said. "It's a Catholic thing."

"Oh," The Huntsman said. "So you are Catholic. I wondered with the prayers and that just now."

Gavin made a sound against his soft palate like fresh gum being scraped from the bottom of a new shoe. Carmelia did not look at her son but at Father Bernard, daring him from behind her sunglasses to make things worse.

"My brother," she said politely, "is a priest."

Over the years, Father Bernard had perfected a meditation on humility, penance and mortification. It was too long to be delivered here. But he did see a beneficial opportunity for bringing its essence to his sister's attention. He placed his hand around his throat just above the soft lapels of the royal-blue golf shift Carmelia had bought him with the recommendation it would be appropriate dress at the resort. Closing his fingers tightly together, he mimed wearing a clerical collar while looking as if he were trying to choke himself to death.

"My sister," he said, "prohibits me appearing as a priest in public."

Removing his hand with the deliberation he would employ correcting a student's error in the ablative case, he added, "Unfortunately."

The Huntsman smiled with perforated obtuseness and seemed to search the far horizon for a sail. Carmelia took off her sunglasses, twirled them in her fingers, returned them to their green leather case, took them out again and put them back on. Father Bernard knew she was trying to summon the waitress, and the bill, through extrasensory indignation. It wasn't working. They might have sat locked there all afternoon, perhaps until it began to snow, had not Gavin rescued his mother.

"Gelato," he said. "Uncle taught me that's the Italian word for ice cream. He said he bought you some in Rome and you loved it. He said I'd love it, too. Could I try some gelato? Could I, please?"

The mockery left The Huntsman even more confused and made Carmelia laugh. It swept over Father Bernard's little victory like a squall.

I am poured out like water, and all my bones are out of joint; my heart is like wax; it is melted in the midst of my bowels; I am like a broken dish...

A broken dish. The words from the Good Friday Psalm were on his tongue when he knocked on Carmelia's door. He did not know what to expect. Not knowing what to expect was becoming part of the condition of a life he wanted just the other way around. Years earlier, accompanying Carmelia on her first trip to the Eternal City, he expected the waiter to bring them coffee. Instead, the mournful, aproned little man appeared with a tray bearing two flowered dishes of icecream. Yellow biscotti jutted out of the caramel-coloured scoops like jaunty paper hats on the heads of children at a birthday party. Across the table, Carmelia, still crying, put her fingers to her lips as if she were about to be sick.

Only moments earlier, they'd escaped the suffocating bus on the Via Aurelia as it lurched toward the Vatican from their lodgings at the Convent of the Sisters of Reparation. Carmelia had broken away from the Roman who'd forced his pinching hands under her skirt.

Separated from his sister by the overheated bodies, Father Bernard had been unable to do anything about the groping. He was unable to get off the bus until two stops after Carmelia had fled. He ran back two blocks to find her sobbing. Seeking to console her over coffee, he was confronted by a morose waiter hovering above them with dishes of celebratory *gelato*.

Gelato. Gelato. Father Bernard started to wave the man away when he realized who had made the mistake. He had. He meant to say *"due caffe, grazie"* but in the confusion of his sister crying, his anger at the assault, his physical dizziness at his own inability to act, he said *"due caffe gelato."* When the order arrived, Carmelia looked at the waiter, then across at her brother. It was all the priest could do to stop from kicking the dishes off the tray before the sad-faced man could set them down.

It was all he could do now to keep from plugging his ears against the risk of rustling sheets and conspiratorial whispers as he knocked on the door of her room. But she was alone. Her floral sundress stuck like a ricochet on the back of the chair. Underwear was clumped on the bed like cleaning clothes left behind by the maid.

She had just showered and was wearing a raspberry-coloured robe, a thick white towel around her wet hair. Her small, square, bare feet reminded him of the baby sister who would sneak out of her bed, tiptoe down the hall and kneel beside him as he said his evening prayers in his room.

"You must stop that," she said.

"Stop what?"

"Judging. You're insufferable when you judge."

She had drawn the blinds but now opened them. Her room faced the side lawn of the resort and had a view of the tennis courts, croquet pitch and bandstand for evening concerts. The sea was around the corner, audible but not visible. The light through the window was a single square pressed flat.

"Judging who? Whom? I didn't say a word about him."

"Exactly."

She scooped the underwear clump into the closet with a single motion, sat on the end of the bed and tilted her head to look at him. She did not invite him to sit down.

He waited by the door, feeling he should have a hat in his hands to fumble with. Even he did not wear a hat anymore. He had stopped after Vatican II when he'd briefly grown fashionable sideburns and a small goatee. Carmelia alarmed him by predicting he'd soon be permitting folk masses in his church. He quickly shaved out of political and theological fidelity to the old order. His hat proved irrecoverable. His housekeeper, Mrs. Hurst, had given it to the Catholic Women's League for a rummage sale. He thought he saw a boy wearing it at a costume party in the school gymnasium.

"Gavin saw you," Carmelia said. "That's what bothers me."

"Saw me? I did nothing. I said nothing. I am not to judge so I say and do nothing."

"He looks up to you. I don't want him to see you doing that."

"I ate my soup."

She tucked her chin to her chest to imitate the timber of his voice. Could her broad mockery be close to what he sounded like?

"My sister, the little harlot, resents me being a priest," she said. "Unfortunately."

He felt he was fending off a single opponent attacking from several directions at once.

"I said no such thing. You don't mind me being a priest. You just don't want me to behave like one. Being versus feeling. Ontology versus psychology."

"Don't," she said, "score points."

"I'm not trying to score points," he said.

"No?"

"No."

"This is a first."

Point scored, she took the towel off her hair, folded it into a neat square, then tossed it into the corner. She had become accustomed to having people pick things up for her. There was hired help in the country home she'd built along the ridge above the weather and the neighbouring fields of corn, hay, and sunflowers.

"I have to get dressed," she said. "We're meeting for drinks."

"Are we?"

"I am."

"Oh. With your new young friend?"

"His name is Tim. Timothy. Like St. Paul's young friend. Isn't it fascinating that even the first priest needed a young friend?"

The insult was so crude Father Bernard was less personally offended than alarmed for his sister. He saw, for an instant only, gathered cruelties nettled in her skin. Then she revived.

"Tim's in fashion," she said. "He's a buyer. He lived in Milan for three years. His Italian is flawless."

Another reference to the accident at the café. What was provoking them now? What had prompted her to tell Gavin the story?

35

For years, it had been left alone as one of those submerged catastrophes that lie under family memory like coral below a swimmer's feet.

A voice on the radio was announcing snow. A blizzard was coming. A tempest. The voice began to speak in impenetrable Italian. Father Bernard could make out only that an elderly couple had died in an auto accident caused by the storm sweeping Rome. He sat up under the bedspread. A night breeze through the open windows was cooling the room.

The red message light on the phone beside the bed was pulsing in the dark, illuminating the wristband of his watch, the coil of his rosary. He delayed picking up the receiver. He swung his legs over the side of the bed and let them dangle as if he were seated on the edge of the pool. He was glad it was dark because he hated the shape of his legs from the knee down, especially the disintegration of his feet as he aged. It frustrated him that people thought the most difficult part of being a priest was being celibate. It was impossible to make them understand sex was only the stage show of vanity.

He thought of Carmelia at the makeup table at the far end of her hotel room during their meeting that afternoon. She was applying eyeliner, squinting into the mirror, when he told her about the special surprise he'd arranged. He'd asked an old friend of his, now the monsignor in charge of the office of patrimony at the Vatican, to give them a private tour – the papal apartments, the back stairs by Bernini, everything. It was all set for the end of their first week in Rome.

She poured a measure of thick, white cream onto her hands and began to rub it into the skin. Its scent made the room smell like overdone dessert. She reminded him that the purpose of the trip was to show Gavin art, not take him to church. Unspoken was the reminder of who was paying for the trip. He protested it was she who had asked him to show her and Gavin around. He was to be their guide, their cicerone.

"You showed me around Rome once, remember," she said. "You bought me ice cream. Caffe gelato. Due caffe gelato."

Her mockery was the mother cloud from which Gavin's sarcasm had dropped. It was too much. For the first time in memory, Father Bernard forgot to retreat.

"So you seem to enjoy telling the world," he said. "Even Gavin got a laugh out of it – at my expense."

"Gavin? What did Gavin say?"

"You heard him at lunch. I'm not sure exactly what you told him. He didn't seem to have the whole story."

"And you gave him the whole story?"

"The part you left out."

"Which was? What did you tell him?"

It was the point to recover his senses. He did not.

"That you enjoyed it."

"It?"

She spat the "t" as if his innuendo were a flying insect on the tip of her tongue.

"Yes," he said. "You enjoyed it. That's my memory. Perhaps it isn't yours."

"What 'it' did I enjoy?" she said. "What 'it' did you tell Gavin I enjoyed?"

She was pouring more cream into her hands. It spread gelatinously.

"The ice cream, of course. The caffe gelato. What else could I have meant?"

She stopped turning her hands over each other and held them up, very still. The patina of fine white cream gave her the air of a gloved surgeon about to cut. Then the hands floated down toward the vanity top as dreamily as the snow he had imagined that afternoon.

"I'm never sure I know what you mean," she said. "I just keep paying for it."

"Only because you want to," he retorted. "The choice is yours."

She looked at him in the mirror so that he had the impression of looking past her to see her in front of herself. He had two sisters. One with her back turned to him. One floating, watching.

"How," she said, "can the choice be mine when the mistakes are yours? Do you think mistakes don't count?"

She resumed rubbing the cream into her hands. He retreated as if kicked. In the elevator, returning to his room, he felt claustrophobic. In his room, lying on his bed, he did not remember falling asleep.

The recorded message when he picked up the phone was from Gavin explaining that his mother had gone into town with her new friend for dinner and asking if Uncle wanted to have something to eat. The message had been left two hours earlier. He phoned his nephew's room. No answer.

His own room was black except for the open window that let in the sound of the sea. He wondered what had become of the old man and the old woman he'd seen quarrelling on the lawn. Who had brought whom here? Who had started the fight with whom? It was so odd. He had only seen them twice in his life, and then for a fleeting instant, yet they had died in one of his dreams.

The pool was supposed to close at 10 p.m. It was after eleven when Father Bernard stood on the veranda looking at tufts of sea in the moonlight and noticed activity under the amber lights behind the iron fence. Walking across the lawn toward it, retracing his steps from that afternoon, he recognized the young waitress from lunch. She'd shed her mannish shorts and t-shirt and wore instead a bright-red maillot. She was bouncing on the diving board.

Her legs, lit from underneath by the wavering lights below the pool surface, showed the sculpted muscles of a competitive swimmer. On the last bounce, she came down on one foot. Her calves and quadriceps tightened synchronously and she catapulted again, her arms circling above her head, Persephone in transit.

In the middle of the pool, a figure wearing a carbuncle-red bathing cap was swimming from side to side with waterbug strokes. As Father Bernard reached the iron fence, he saw it was the old woman. The old man, still in his black suit and heavy shoes, sat on a chaise longue a few feet from where she touched the wall and turned. He rose and approached the gate as Father Bernard reached it.

"Are you looking for your son?" the man asked. "He was sitting there drawing for a while, but he left. The girl there said it would be all right if my wife went for a late swim. Your boy followed us in."

He gestured toward the young woman just as she arced into the air again. The priest half expected her to simply continue rising until she disappeared into the night sky. He was half-disappointed when she plummeted back into the water. He looked at the old man.

"He's my nephew. Did you see where he went?"

"He was drawing pictures. Of her."

He surprised the priest by inclining his head toward the old woman skittering from side to side as though she feared someone or something would force her to finish before she was ready. Her form was appalling to as skilled a swimmer as Father Bernard. Yet in an odd way it emphasized her endurance, made her seem indefatigable. Somehow, that reassured him about Gavin. The boy was not much physically yet, but there was a surprising durability to him that would develop outside and in.

"Maybe he's down on the beach drawing the midnight moon," Father Bernard laughed. "He's got a gift."

The young woman was on the board again. The old woman showed no sign of tiring.

"Kids get upset by arguments. The next day they can't even remember what it was all about," the old man said.

His face was waxy under the amber lights. The sluice of the

water at the periphery of the priest's vision created the illusion that the nose, the slack lips, the pouched cheeks might melt.

"Argument?" Father Bernard said. "What argument?"

It was the man's turned to be surprised.

"I saw you at lunch," he said. "On the patio. You and your wife. I could tell there had been some kind of argument."

It was an honest mistake, the kind people made when their minds were preoccupied. Obviously absorbed by his own argument with his wife, the man had looked at strangers on the patio and assumed they, too, were husband and wife quarrelling.

"She's not my wife," Father Bernard said. "She's my sister. I'm a priest."

The man bobbed back as though a soggy, sand-covered beach ball had been lobbed at his head. He apologized several times even though the priest held up his hand and said it was unnecessary.

"The boy seemed upset," he said. "I just assumed."

Father Bernard said he'd better go and look for his nephew. But he remained with his elbows propped on the top of the iron gate. The man interested him. Gavin was a careful boy. He was probably already in his room in bed.

The young woman broke the surface from beneath the water, climbed out of the pool in shimmering light and stood at the side towelling off. The elderly woman flipped onto her back and, alone in the water, did a kind of spastic backstroke that left her half-submerged.

"You had an argument, too," the priest said. "I heard you on the lawn with your wife this morning. She seemed very angry. I'm not asking you to tell me what it was about."

The man regained the step he'd lost. He did not, as Father Bernard feared he might, adopt the tone of a penitent behind the confessional screen. Instead he spoke with a bluntness that would have been a bark except he was chuckling.

"What are you asking me then?" he said. "What do you need

to know?"

Father Bernard could not remember when he'd last been asked the question so directly. Almost from childhood, it seemed, people had come to him for answers, usually with oblique requests for advice that they then ignored, avoiding him afterward as a result. He waited before speaking in case he was never asked again.

"How you resolved it," he said finally. "What you said."

"He said he was sorry. Usually, that's all it takes. You should try it. More men should. More husbands."

The old woman spoke from the edge of the pool. She was holding on to the side, resting her floating weight on her astonishingly long arms. Her carbuncle-red hat bobbed like a marker buoy. The man turned to her, fluttering a hand as though waving a caution flag.

"She's not his wife," he said. "They're not married. It's not his son. She's his sister. He's a priest."

The woman brought bottle-cap knees up against the pool, then pushed off with her feet, rocking out to the middle of the pool and slowly swimming back in again. When she reached the side she shook her head to dislodge the water from her ears.

"Who knew?" she said.

"You could ask before interrupting," the old man said.

"You were talking about me. I have a right to defend myself."

"Defend? What's to defend? He asked me a question. I was answering."

"Don't shout."

"Who's shouting?"

"Now you're shouting. You can't hear yourself."

"If I can hear you, I can hear myself. Sometimes I don't hear anything but you."

"Rude. Cruel. Apologize. Who asked you to come here?"

"I'm sorry."

The old woman began to pull herself out of the water. She paused part way and looked up at Father Bernard.

"You see?" she said. "Easy."

Father Bernard looked down at her: at the breasts oozing like old cooking grease out of the bathing-suit front, at the withered skin on the long arms.

"So I'm told," he said.

It was after midnight when he reached the Cape Cod veranda again. He was so lost in thought he almost walked past Gavin, who sat in one of the old wicker chairs, looking grumpy, his sketchbook slipping out from under an arm.

"I was looking for you," Father Bernard said. "Where did you go?"

"Along the beach," Gavin said. "I was watching the moon."

It came out like the admission of a minor sin: stealing candy, pulling a cat's tail.

"You can see the moon from here."

"I like the way the waves make the light move."

His tone held the kind of lapse that occurs when a boy moving forward fast to adult-hood reverses and becomes a momentary child again. Father Bernard felt the urge to carry him on his hip upstairs as if he were a toddler. It was a moment he wanted to hold.

"Any new drawings?" he asked. "Anything to show me?"

It was meant as an invitation, but Gavin sat up straight as if being challenged. He straightened the slipping sketchbook under his arm protectively.

"They're not finished," he said. "They're no good."

"Never let perfection be the enemy of the good."

It came out sounding idiotic. Inept. Gavin looked up at him.

I am poured out like water, my heart is like wax, Father Bernard thought. In Matthew's Gospel, the rich young man walks away insulted after Christ tells him to give up everything. Yet no one ever criticized the Messiah for saying the wrong thing and driving off a potential convert. The priest looked across the lawn at the waxy lights reflecting on the surface of the empty pool.

"You should go to bed," he said. "Sleep in tomorrow. I'll tell your mother we were up late together."

"I'm going to wait for her here," Gavin said. "She's not back yet."

"Then I," Father Bernard said, "will wait with you."

Gavin balanced his book on the arm of the chair for the second time that day. There was no possibility of mistaking the look on his face for amusement. He was not weighing a taste. He was settling loyalties.

"It might look," he said, "as if we're both mad at her."

The priest's legs felt so weak he was afraid he might topple over if he did not sit down. He lowered himself into one of the porch chairs. His temptation was to take Gavin through a discussion proving neither of them was really angry with Carmelia, that disagreement and anger were separate, if related, phenomena. He resisted.

"Your mother, he said instead, "is my sister. I love her as much as you do, albeit in a different form. I think the two people who love her should wait for her to return, don't you?"

Gavin shrugged, signalling acceptance of the *fait accompli*: his uncle was already sitting down. Father Bernard settled back against the overstuffed cushion and tried to think of something more to say. But no. There was nothing. Cricks in his neck muscles made him aware that he was dozing off.

He woke up to the harsh early light and the sound of a heavy tide. He'd been dreaming about Carmelia dancing with the morose waiter in a white room above a Roman café. He was alone on the porch. There was dew on his clothing, his unshaven face and the fine hairs along his arms. Gavin was gone.

It was 36 hours before the boy's body washed up on the shore miles from the resort, past the former president's summer retreat, in a small cove where local teenagers went to sunbathe and drink canned beer. He had been swept out by the undertow of the tide. A middle-aged couple in the honeymoon suite had been on their balcony drinking champagne and eating fresh fruit when they saw him splashing in the breakers at dawn. Father Bernard agreed to make the identification at the morgue. Timothy offered to drive.

"I keep thinking it's a dream," Timothy said as they got into the car. "I keep thinking I'll wake up and he'll be all right."
The car's interior was stifling. Father Bernard began to sweat the moment he closed the door. He had barely slept since waking to find Gavin missing. He felt as if he were in a crawl space, hunched, confined, separated. It was as if his quarrel with Carmelia, his odd moments with the elderly couple, Gavin's sketch of the diver were all above him, irretrievable, scattered across the floor of a room he could never re-enter.

And Carmelia? She was still in her room at the resort, comatose with sedatives and disbelief. What would happen when she had to come out?

"Could you put down a window, please?" Father Bernard asked. "It's difficult to breathe."

Timothy pushed a button on a console and the window beside the priest disappeared. Instead of bringing relief, the sea-smell of the air was like the stench of rotting fish

"I said I would wait with him. I fell asleep."

It appalled him to make the confession to an American he had only met two days before. It horrified him to rely on the superficial kindness of this particular stranger. But there was no one else. He brought his hand to his lips.

Timothy stopped the car in front of the morgue. A boy walked past leading a ridiculous mongrel on a red leash. At the corner, the mutt stopped to cock a leg at a fire hydrant. Then it sat down and scratched an ear. The boy waited philosophically.

"Look at him," Father Bernard said.

He found the handle of the car door, pulled it up and swung his legs out. Timothy came around the hood to the passenger side solicitously. He directed a hand toward the priest's elbow, as if helping a frail grandfather. But Father Bernard pulled himself out. He stood up alone. The movement of rising too quickly made blood rush from his head and he felt, briefly, light, almost buoyant. If he could do nothing else, he would find the strength to walk by himself to the room where his nephew lay on a stainless-steel gurney covered by a clean white sheet. He would pray over the body for the repose of the departed soul.

Yom Kippur

Taylor's life was not so great, but he was still able that Saturday morning to be out raking the September leaves off his lawn. He was even okay pausing, here and there, to flick curly-cues of dried dog shit into the gutter with the red tines of his rake. He would have bet twenty dollars it was against the law in Hamilton for people to let their dogs take a dump on other people's lawns. Still, it happened, and he was able, raking as he was, to work around it without feeling that someone had necessarily put the dog shit there on purpose.

Sometimes, Taylor did feel certain people did certain things on purpose. He could, when he was busy with a mindless task, go off into himself thinking about why certain kinds of certain people did the same certain things all the time, as if there was something in their genes making them do it. He could spend hours wondering why they aimed certain things at him in particular. Other times, he came back to realizing most of what people did was not because of the certain group they belonged to but because of pure thoughtlessness – obliviousness was the word he would use in his own head though not out loud since it sounded a little too la-di-da for the way most people spoke.

He scooped the red and yellow leaves against the rake tines with one hand and dumped them into the green canvas collection bag and carried the bag to the compost Sherry had started in May when she and that whack-job Catholic woman she worked with had got the bright idea to start a community garden not just for their neighbours on Young Street but for their whole neighbourhood of Corktown. The whole garden project had flopped right out of the gate, as Taylor had warned it might, but he was keeping his promise to keep composting in case the bright idea came back to Sherry and the Catholic whack-job woman next spring. It seemed unlikely, given the way life was going, but there was always hope. If life was not so great for Taylor, he knew of other lives that were worse. It did not make him feel great that other lives were worse. It let him rake his lawn. It let him hope.

What was not so great was that Sherry was in Winnipeg staying with a couple she'd known since the University of Manitoba. She said she needed time out and that was understandable. She had the kids with her. It was better that Tyler and Tammy were with her. Kids should be with their mom. Still, there was the always ready worry that the time Sherry needed out was so indefinite it might suddenly never end.

He had the right to relieve his worry, didn't he? He folded the canvas collection bag carefully and put it in its proper spot on the back porch and went in the house. He called Winnipeg even though, technically, he wasn't supposed to call so soon after the last call. There was one of those long silences between the time that the man of the University of Manitoba couple – Jerry? Benjamin? – answered the phone and called out Sherry's name and Sherry picked up what sounded like a downstairs receiver. The silence was filled with what sounded like somebody assembling lawn furniture but was probably someone filling the dishwasher with breakfast dishes. Taylor thought he heard his name mentioned under the scuff of a throat clearing just before Sherry picked up.

"No pressure," he said. He honestly meant it as the words came out of his mouth. The kids couldn't come to the phone because they were watching cartoons. After he hung up, all Taylor could think to do was walk from the kitchen to the living room and then on into the bedroom to look out the window at the lawn he had just raked. He went back to the kitchen. On the front of the fridge were Tammy's drawings of pink and purple unicorns that seemed modelled on half-eaten onion rings. He admired them. Then he thought about the time of day. He actually felt relieved it was way too early to even think about having one of the beers in the fridge.

He noticed a yellow-red leaf had somehow worked its way under the laces of his left shoe, and wondered how it got there without him noticing. In the bathroom, he took his watch from the soap dish where he'd left it while he was shaving and showering. He questioned why women buy pink shower curtains featuring fluffy blue kittens wearing yellow wizard's hats. He agreed with himself it would be okay to have one beer today. As long as he drank just the one beer with deliberation and purpose, as a break in the middle of his chores for the day, it was as reasonable as it was reasonable for Sherry to be back in Winnipeg with her old friends.

When she told him she was going back to the Pearl of the Prairies for the time out, he knew it was purely because of the friends. It made no sense otherwise for her to want to go back there of all places. Even she admitted it was awful what was happening to Winnipeg these days.

Even before they were uprooted and forced to move away from the Pearl of the Prairies, even before Taylor had his job taken from him by those Rich Media Mogul Jews he worked for, even before Sherry had quit her nursing job for the move to Hamilton, things were getting bad in Winnipeg. Even she agreed, looking back, it was lucky, in a weird way, for them to get out of there and move to Hamilton when they did.

The truth was they got out just as those Rich Media Mogul Jews – Taylor would not speak their family name after what they did to him – and Native gangs were dividing Winnipeg up between them, top and bottom, and boning it hard in the mouth and up the ass at the same time. It might be different holes and different dicks but they all were getting their money shots just the same. That was on purpose. They knew what they were doing. Yes they did.

The true reason for what was happening to Winnipeg, a truth even Sherry would not admit, was something Taylor kept inside his head and would not dare to say out loud even in his own home. Rich Powerful Winnipeg Jews Who Own All the Newspapers In The Country And Treat Employees Like Shit were not words anyone could speak out loud in Canada anymore. It could be worth someone's job, especially someone's politically sensitive job in the communications department at the regional authority in Hamilton, to tell the truth in public about what The Rich Winnipeg Jews were doing by deliberately taking jobs away and forcing loyal, long-serving employees to move across the country just to find work and be able to feed their kids. Taylor wasn't the only one they hurt. Even Sherry admitted that.

It wasn't Jews in general he had anything against. Au contraire. When he worked for the Rich Media Jews in Winnipeg, he worked with a Jew named Judith Eisenberg, and he liked working with her a lot. She brought latkes once to the department Christmas potluck lunch and Taylor thought they were delicious and him liking them led to them discussing Jewish customs and culture, which led to her explaining to him why she took time off every September for the holiest day of the Jewish year, Yom Kippur. The way she explained it made it sound to him like Easter in September without the blood and miracles.

The Hebrew words translated as The Day of Atonement, and it was a day when Judith and her family walked around with stones in their pockets to throw into still water as atonement for their sins. He walked around for a week or so afterward with an image in his mind of Judith Eisenberg's small hand cupped full of grey and black pebbles, turning outward as her arm moved in an arc across her body from her ribcage to her opposite hip.

He went by her desk and joked with her one morning that maybe next Yom Kippur he could go with her and they could throw rocks at their boss's big boat. She had just hung up the phone when he came by and didn't seem to get what he was saying at first and then said "what?" After that came the job cuts. Still, Taylor could say sincerely that Judith Eisenberg throwing stones into still water made more sense to him, religiously, than that whack-job Catholic woman and her nut-bar Catholic husband Sherry had invited over for dinner only to have them sit at his table and claim the bread and wine actually turned into the actual body and blood of Jesus on Sunday mornings.

No, it was not ordinary Jews. It wasn't Judith Eisenberg Jews. It was the rich and powerful Winnipeg Jews, their job-cutting and their political propaganda control of Canada's newspapers and other media that frightened – he might sometimes silently say infuriated – him.

As for the Native gangs that were banging the city for money shots, who would want to screw with them?

Back in the kitchen, looking at his watch, he took the beer from the fridge. Just one. Even with Sherry away and things being what they were and life not being so great, Taylor wasn't going to let that get out of control again. He bent and took the yellow and red leaf from between his shoe laces and held it crumbling in the fingers of the hand that wasn't holding the beer and went outside to sit on his front step and watch Young Street, where Tyler and Tammy could set out without fear each day to go to school. Or least without fear that was more than the usual fear that was a normal part of the frightening of young kids going to school and growing up.

Tyler might be afraid of getting another D in arithmetic and Tammy might be afraid that her skinny pony legs would always be skinny pony legs, but neither of them had to fear being kidnapped by rapist pedophiles as they walked home from Shamrock Park through the tunnel under the old THB railway tracks. At least they had never mentioned they were afraid of rapist pedophiles in the THB tunnel, though Taylor thought maybe he should, at some point, have asked them directly. He realized he did not know what, apart from the usual fears of childhood, his children were afraid of. It started the worry up again that he would never actually get the chance to speak to them again, depending on what Sherry decided to do and, it had to be admitted, what was possibly really going on in the Pearl of the Prairies.

Here came, then, the daily struggle to not call Sherry at her friends' place just one more time that day or send her just one more e-mail saying he just wanted to know how she was doing and make sure everything was okay with the kids. If he did, there would come again his saying "no pressure" in all its variations ("I'm sorry if it seems like I'm pressuring you; I don't mean to pressure you; I just miss you that's all; no, I want you to take the time you need to decide without feeling any pressure; no, don't feel pressured to come home just for me; don't come home until you have decided that you are ready...") and then would come the horrible, frightening emptiness of lying in his and Sherry's bed wondering all night whether he had made things worse.

The worst part of all this was that it was not what he ever imagined would be the thing that happened to him. Taylor's one fear growing up, beyond the usual fears of being a kid, was that nothing would ever really happen to him. Nothing ever seemed to. Yes, he met Sherry in Winnipeg and married her, and after the Rich Media Jews cut jobs the only choice was to move to Hamilton to the little house they could afford in Corktown, so-called because of all the poverty-stricken Irish immigrants who came fleeing the Potato Famine in the 1840s, and, true, he had restarted his career by getting the job at the regional authority, created Tyler and Tammy with Sherry and was raising them and sending them off to school safely every morning.

Even the Rich Powerful Jews taking away his job wasn't something that happened to him per se. It was something being done deliberately to everyone they wielded their power over. It was just life unfolding. Life in a world run by Rich Powerful Jews.

Things happening were things like the time, once, in the small BC town where he grew up, that a sky-blue bus full of mentally retarded kids was hit right on the corner of his street by a logging truck that lost its brakes coming down Eighth Avenue to the pulp mill, and his dad helped carry some of the kids from the wreckage of the bus into a house across the street. Even there, Taylor was in his room when it happened, and even though the bang brought him to the window, when he looked out all he could see was the sky-blue bus lying on its side as if the sky itself had slipped down from where it should be, and his mother wouldn't let him go outside to look closer and, in fact, made him go and play in the bedroom at the back of the house that she shared with Taylor's father.

In the morning, the only thing he heard his father say was "blood all over my hands" before his parents stopped talking when he came into the kitchen. He was too young at the time to buy the local newspaper to find out what happened. His father wouldn't allow it in the house anyway because he didn't like the family that owned it. So, outside Taylor's bedroom window, at the corner of the street where he lived, mentally retarded kids on their way back to their institution from their weekly outing to the bowling alley and the A&W had been killed, but it had not actually happened to him. It was just something he saw a small part of, late.

He sat for a long time on his porch watching the September vegetation die on the rock face of the Niagara Escarpment that ran all the way from Wisconsin in the west and somehow miraculously dove right under the Great Lakes and even more miraculously popped up right there, right in front of him, a small mountain of layers of flaking grey-and-black shale looming over his tiny neighbourhood of

Corktown before plunging to become the vast, black, roaring gorge of Niagara Falls and, even after expending all that energy, continue to stretch for miles and miles and more miles as far as Watertown, New York. There was something good about the escarpment. There was something good and hopeful, too, about Young Street and Corktown and his house, and that something good and hopeful would bring Sherry and Tyler and Tammy back. It would be okay. He could have one more afternoon beer. It would be okay. Nothing was going to happen. He crumbled the red-and-yellow leaf into tiny dry bits and tried to toss the handful of the bits away, but his wrist motion was clumsy and they just made a small mess on the knees of his jeans.

When he and Sherry were moving from Winnipeg to Hamilton – from one forgotten Canadian city to another – after his job-loss fiasco and her having to let go of her nursing job, Taylor had the idea that everyone in their new city would be beefy Italians working as steel workers at Stelco or Dofasco. Wrong. They were not beefy. They were fat. Not just fat Italians but fat every bodies everywhere he looked: fat black people, fat natives, fat young welfare mothers pushing strollers along King Street East, fat blonde executive assistants in the regional authority office, fat panhandlers around the bus depot on Hunter Street. What kind of downtown has fat panhandlers? A downtown that everyone in southern Ontario drives past on the way to Toronto or London.

There were, of course, fat Jews, too. Not too many fat Jews, not as many as in Winnipeg, but a few. One such fat Jew ran the little café that Taylor was sitting in at the corner of King East and Walnut Street. Taylor was not paying attention to the Jew or anything else in the café. He knew the café. He brought Tyler and Tammy there sometimes on Friday nights while Sherry was doing the grocery shopping. Sometimes he came alone when Sherry was in one of her imitation Catholic-martyr moods and quiet was the only thing that could cut the coming fight off at the knees. He would sit in a back booth and watch the Molson's Canadian clock on the wall at the far end of the counter until it was Sherry's usual bedtime and the house was guaranteed to be safely dark when he got home. Tonight, Taylor was not watching the clock. He was looking out the window at fat men walking down King East toward the massage parlour he knew was still tucked away on Wentworth Street.

Cops in Hamilton still raided massage parlours from time to time. Taylor knew this because he had been tempted, no, not just tempted but had actually worked himself up to go to the massage parlour and there had been a raid and as he walked past there were cop cars, unmarked ones and also regular cop cars with their light bars spinning blue and red dance ball illumination across the front of the building and he hurried by and went home and felt the right thing to do was to truthfully tell Sherry what he had so narrowly avoided. He never imagined she would be so devastated by him even being tempted. He was stunned when she brought up, and tied in, all the other things she said had happened, which at first he did not even know where they were coming from or how they had anything to do with what he had told her about. It dawned on him late in the fight that he was an idiot and should have kept his mouth shut. About doing the right thing at the massage parlour. About everything.

When they started speaking again a few days later, he knew he needed to seek forgiveness and thought of Judith Eisenberg and Yom Kippur and he thought he could show Sherry how sorry he was, and also show Tyler and Tammy how other cultures said they were sorry, by grouping everybody in their small kitchen between the back door and the refrigerator, and by reaching into the small spice cupboard above the stove and pouring out some ground black pepper into one hand to simulate Day of Atonement stones, and tossing them into the sink he'd filled with cold water. It came off as ridiculous, and Taylor put the pepper back in the cupboard harder than he meant to and that knocked all the other spice bottles and cans tumbling all over the kitchen floor and, yes, that pissed him off.

Tyler backed up right against the fridge. Tammy crouched down below her drawings on the fridge door and tugged the hem of her dress as if she was trying to pull it down to her ankles. Sherry said, after the kids went up to their rooms, that Taylor's little show was worse than ridiculous. It was ridiculing, she said, and probably sacrilegious.

She'd noticed how ignorantly he'd been treating other people, including her Catholic friends, for quite a while and Tyler was starting to use some of the same horrible language about people that Taylor used, and she wasn't sure who her husband was anymore, and she needed time out while she thought about what it meant for their marriage. By "it," she meant everything including the massage parlour episode that, technically, she had forgiven. She meant him.

So nothing had happened and yet he had tried to atone, and still he had screwed it up royally and now there he was alone, slightly drunk from the two or so beers that afternoon, though the good part was that he was sitting safely in the fat Jew's café eating a white-bread sandwich supper and drinking one more beer on a Saturday night, and he could sit there safely until it closed. It was not the greatest place to be sitting alone on a Saturday night, but it was better than being in a bar drinking beer after beer and getting drunker than he was from the two or so afternoon beers, and a whole lot better than being in that massage parlour getting a hand job as the cops busted in.

He turned his head toward the focus point of the sound of a fat hand slapping the far end of the counter at the front of the café. A portable TV on a high shelf behind the cash register showed the Leafs losing yet again. Players in red-white-and-blue jerseys – effing Montreal – were high-fiving gloves along the visitors' bench.

"Christ," the owner said. "What a bunch of losers. Loser Leafs. That's what I call them. My loser Leafs."

The score was either 3-1 or 8-1. It was impossible to tell from Taylor's angle and distance. Still, did the Jew have to say Christ? Taking the Lord's name in vain like that? Not good. Not good from a fat Jew. Not good from anybody, but especially not from a fat Jew.

"Hey," Taylor said. "Language, eh?"

The owner looked down the distance of the café toward him, past the black-leather dress jacket of a man in a blue-and-white Blue Jays hat who was sitting at the counter reading the *National Post*. Taylor meant his correction to be mild and friendly and fellow suffering, as though to someone who had just stubbed his toe. He even glanced at the bench across from him as if Tammy were there finishing up a plate of fish and chips and Tyler was wolfing down the house specialty Whoa-Whoa Burger.

"Sorry," the owner said. "I get upset when my loser Leafs lose."

"Your problem," Taylor said, "is not being a Bruins fan."

Friendly again, and forgiving, but even he heard how the beer-bubbled excess between his tongue and lips made "Bruins" sound like a spit wad. The owner did not continue the banter. The man in the leather jacket did not look over or even up, either. It was as if he and the Jew were in on it together, that accidental, but also sometimes deliberate, ignoring of Taylor that so many people seemed to have down to a T.

Reaching into his coat pocket, the man took out a pack of cigarettes and lit one. He turned the pages of his *Post* as studiously as Taylor had pretended to study Scripture during his eager evangelical days, those days before he got bored hearing the same thing over and over every Sunday morning and every Wednesday evening at men's Bible study circle. Smoke from the cigarette plumed toward a small circular ceiling vent. The man took a drag, looked around for an ashtray and, not finding one, balanced the cigarette on the edge of the counter as if it were some kind of small animal he had taught a minor trick.

"You can't do that," Taylor said.

He called it out. He heard himself. But he was justified. He was justified and there was no reason it should lead to trouble. He was within his rights. The man turned toward him. He looked like a beefy Italian who would be a fat Italian any day. He was already developing a fat Italian face.

"Is it bothering you?" the man said.

He moved the cigarette to his other side, blocking the smoke with his body, though it still plumed above his head toward the ceiling vent. Taylor sniffed the air. Whatever he could or couldn't smell was beside the point.

"It's illegal," he said. "You can't smoke in restaurants."

"It's not bothering you," the man said.

The café owner put his fat hand on the man's arm. There it was again, the ganging up. Taylor saw the owner twist his chicken-skin lips to one side and shake his head. The man said something and the owner obediently got the coffee pot and refilled the man's mug. From under the counter, he brought out a glass ashtray that looked as if it had been stolen from the bar of the Royal Connaught Hotel 30 years before. He set it on the counter. The man put the cigarette between his lips.

"Put it out, retard," Taylor said.

He hadn't really said something so childish, had he? Surely someone else had set the sentence on short stocky legs to walk like a belligerent 17-year-old down the distance of the café. It wasn't him. It could not have been him. But no. It was.

"What did you say?" the man said.

"There's no need for that," the owner said.

He said it to Taylor. Obviously, Taylor was on the outside, the bad guy, as always. Sherry would have acted the same. She would have automatically taken the side against him. Her shoulders would have risen up as though she was going stand up to walk out, and he would have to talk her into staying until he finished his coffee.

"Are you some kind of mental retard?" Taylor said. "You can't smoke in here. Make him stop or I call the cops."

He fished his Blackberry out of his pocket and looked down at the keypad as though counting off seconds before calling 9-1-1. The owner nudged the ashtray and the man took the cigarette out of his mouth and stubbed it. He shifted his weight back slightly on the counter stool and spun toward nine on the clock face of the otherwise empty café.

"Have you got some kind of a problem?" he said.
He folded his *National Post*. He was fat, not beefy. He didn't look like he'd ever worked in the steel for Stelco or Dofasco.

"Have I got some kind of a problem?" Taylor said. "My problem is that you were smoking illegally. That's my only problem."

It sounded untrue even to Taylor. The man shook his head. The deep-blue bill of the Blue Jay's cap moved back and forth in the small motions of a cleaning cloth erasing. Taylor saw how fat, not beefy, he was and he knew he could take him if it came to it. Taylor had taken tae kwon do for almost a year and worked out on a heavy bag several times a week in college. Fuck fear. He was ready now to go if anything got going. The man turned back and looked at the café owner.

"What are you putting in that guy's beer, Pillows?" he said. "Whatever it is, don't give him any more."

Pillows? Was the owner's name really Pillows? It had to be a nickname. The fat Italian and the fatter Jew were nickname friends. Nickname friends. Taylor was outraged at being outnumbered and, worse, unnamed.

"Why don't you say that to me?" he said.

His challenge made no sense. It was the only thing he could think of to say. Another round of high-fiving was going on at the visitors' bench on the TV screen. The man took out three loonies to pay

59

for his coffee. He lined them up down the spine of his folded *National Post*. He swivelled to three o'clock, his broad leather back aimed at Taylor.

"Why don't you ask our friend there to calm down, Pillows?" he said.

He broke the last consonant off "friend" deliberately, as deliberately as if he were asking someone why someone else had put dog shit under his shoe. Taylor got ready. Something was coming. Something was going to happen. He would make it happen.

"Why don't you shove your Jewspaper up your ass?" he said.

Had he said it? Had he really said it? No. He had yelled it. It had come ripping and jumping out of him, green and grinning and answering to the name of poltergeist as it ran forward pell-mell.

"My what?" the man said. "Did that asshole just say what I think that asshole just said?"

Pillows stood very still. He was looking past the man's shoulder at Taylor, and Taylor could see Pillows saw something coming, too.

"I said it," Taylor said. "You heard me. You've been sitting there reading that Jewspaper like it's a real newspaper. Everybody knows that shit rag is owned by Winnipeg Jews who fill their Jewspapers with their Jew news while they treat Canadians like shit. Everybody but you, retard."

Was he waving his arms? His arms were waving. A second poltergeist was ripping his voice box. Something was going to come now, and he was ready to go when it went. Something would fly and there would be smashing glass and things being thrown around and things lying on their sides on the floor of the café and Taylor and the man or Taylor and Pillows or Taylor taking them both on rolling around on the floor punching and kicking and eye-gouging and noses bloodying and eyes blackening and ribs cracking and Taylor would drive punches deep into one fat face and then the other fat face

60

and cops would come and pull him victorious off the pile and everything would be shattered, shattered, smashed to smithereens. What
would Sherry say about the smithereens he'd created? Face bloodied,
he would stand up and laugh at her use of the word smithereens and
say it sounded like something someone in Corktown would say right
after they got off the boat from fleeing the Potato Famine, and her not
even being Irish but bohunk Winnipeg Ukrainian.

Pillows came down and stood at Taylor's table. His belly
bulged under his white shirt and hung over the black belt holding up
the grease-grey pants. He had grey and black curly hair sprung over
his ears. He had grey and black bristle hair in his nostrils. His breath
rasped, too, yet he was so calm. He picked up the broken white plate
that was cracked in half on Taylor's table. Pieces of white bread tomato
sandwich were scattered over the yellow Arborite.

"Look," Pillows said, "you need to calm down. There's no need
for this."

"You need to tell your friend over there to fuck off," Taylor
said.

He was saying it out loud. Even the fuck off part. He left out
the "Jews news" part on purpose, looking into Pillows' face. But he
had told him to tell the friend to fuck off. He made his right hand into
a fist. It was coming.

"Maybe so," Pillows said. "But this is my place of business. I
own it. If I tell one customer to fuck off, who knows where it might
lead? My kids have to eat."

Expecting to be struck, Taylor was instead stuck. Stuck. Pillows had outsmarted him by refusing to fight. It was what Taylor did
to Sherry when he walked out and went elsewhere during her Catholic martyr phases when silence was the only way to cut the coming
fight off at the knees. He had been outsmarted – given a taste of his
own medicine – by a Jew who wouldn't fight. And by Sherry, too. It
was what she had done after the massage parlour fiasco by going back

to the Pearl of the Prairies for a time out. By a Jew, and by Sherry, too.

"You shouldn't have let him smoke," Taylor said.

"The sandwich is on me," Pillows said. "And the beer. You need me to call you a cab?"

He picked up the empty beer bottles, one with its Molson Canadian label half picked off. Taylor's Blackberry buzzed on the tabletop. Someone was sending him e-mail. He rooted in his pocket and pulled out a twenty and a ten for the beer and the crappy tomato sandwich. He didn't need a Jew's charity.

"Keep the change," he said.

Standing up, he grabbed the peppershaker and began furiously shaking pepper out through the perforations in the dented silver top. When it didn't come fast enough, he twisted the top off and dumped the pepper all over the white bread and the yellow Arborite. It was a half-assed attempt at nothing. It got him nowhere.

"You should go now," Pillows said.

Taylor's last chance, opening the door to leave, was that the fat Italian would call him a fascist or a Nazi or a something that would spin his shoulders around and march him back inside, justified fists blazing. He didn't. It wasn't coming. It was over. Nothing had happened. He had just suffered a humiliating piss pounding all the same.

Things got worse. He leaned against the front wall of Thompson's pawnshop, under its red and yellow awning, in the dark of the corner of Walnut Street and King East. He watched a drunken, emaciated, sexually ambiguous teenager come fast out of the Brickyard Bar across the street, then struggle to pull open the door of the body piercing parlour two doors down. A young woman with gecko eyes, pimpled facial skin, and pants pulled down to show her pink and yellow thong picked at things in the air in front of the Dollar Store. Taylor was shaking, trying to breathe in enough already cooling air from the wind coming off Hamilton bay to let him come back to his real self.

His knees were weak and he felt as if his legs might give way and part of him hoped they would so he could crawl over to the edge of the sidewalk and puke his guts out, puke not just the beer in his guts out of his guts into the gutter but puke out his guts themselves, actually puke himself out of himself, puke away the human being who had deliberately tried, and pathetically failed, to pick a humiliating fight by saying unspeakable things in a public place to people he didn't even know. He was full of beer and as empty as a money shot in a massage parlour.

It could not get worse than this, and even that was not true. He could make it worse. He could find a way. It wasn't that something had gotten into him. It was that it was already there, and he had wanted to bring it out. It was who he was, a piece of shit, and why Sherry was in Winnipeg and why Tyler and Tammy weren't at home getting up every morning to walk safely up Young Street to school. He started to walk with nowhere to go but home, which was empty too.

He should have gone straight up Walnut. Instead, he took the long way around. He wandered back up King. At the parkade entrance for the Crowne Plaza, he crossed paths with a crack head panhandler and gave him ten dollars and then gagged not at the crack head's acid-burn smell but at his own lameness in trying to buy some kind of decency back. Just past the abandoned hulk of the Royal Connaught Hotel, a bunch of native men were passing around a brown paper bag and they laughed as he went by, and he got out his Blackberry again and stared into it so it looked like he really was deliberately ignoring them and not just pretending to ignore them.

And the e-mail was from Sherry. E-mails. Two of them. Not just one. He had missed the second buzz when the Blackberry was in his pocket while he was outside in the dark leaning against the pawnshop wall. Now his hands were shaking the way his whole body had been shaking. He thumb-clicked the second message first.

SUBJECT LINE: Can you call?

MESSAGE: Hope its not too late or that I havent missed you.
TIME: 10:58:42.

Ninety minutes before. Or something like 90 minutes. And then there was the time change. Was Winnipeg two hours ahead? Or two hours behind? Who could figure out time, time zones, digital time, anyway?

It was too long ago anyway. He would have missed her anyway. She would be in bed now in her friends' house in the Pearl of the Prairies, Tyler and Tammy maybe snuggled beside her, anyway. He was going to write back anyway to leave her a message for the morning but checked the first message first just in case something in it made it better for him not to write at all.

SUBJECT LINE: Just to say
MESSAGE: I do love you, you know. I still realy do.
TIME: 10:26:33

He thumb rolled the messages back and forth on the screen, reading them as he was walking. She still did love him. Mysteriously, she still really did. She had wanted him to call. No pressure. Just talk. He scrolled the lines out the bottom of the Blackberry screen and then brought them back again, making them come and go like surprise gifts in their tiny glass box. Talk to say what? To say whatever came after I do love you, you know. I still realy do.

He began walking home to Corktown, to Young Street, scrolling, reading what Sherry had written, praying please-please-please to the God he had lost interest in on Wednesday evenings that Sherry would still want to talk to him in the morning, would still want to say what came after I still love you, would still love him.

He was still scrolling in the crosswalk at the corner of Hunter and John. The GO bus was just pulling out of the station trying to make the light to make time on the night's last run to Toronto, and Taylor looked up just in time to take two enormous-legged strides to dive out of its path to avoid being hit by it and dove right into the path of the red step side pickup truck passing in the right lane as its driver made the run to pick up coffee and donuts from Tim Horton's for herself and her night-shift workmates.

The bumper and grill of the pickup caught him fair and square and full in the ribs and hip and spun him around and launched him toward the sidewalk on the far side of Hunter, a point on the map of the world that he floated toward with his arms and legs outstretched to guide him through the slow-motion turns he was making in a life where it no longer mattered whether the forces acting on him were deliberate or thoughtless or oblivious or whether he was a pearl or a piece of shit or whether he was a Gentile or a Jew or whether he was in the gutter or in the pile of yellow and red leaves on the grass, alive, unhurt, injured, dead. Injured, dead would happen sooner or later anyway. It was a matter of timing and waiting.

But something else seemed already, as he spun, to be happening and life… life seemed to be turning, gracefully turning, on its own axis, like a pocketful of stones thrown out in a slow, atoning arc over still water. That was what he could know, all he could know, for sure.

If Only

Angie's quilted blue bathrobe gapes when she pours coffee at the kitchen counter and again as she brings the cups to the table and bends to set one in front of Grant. He thinks about possibilities and how it is best that there is no possibility at all.

"What time," he says, "do you start work?"

It is the Monday morning of his weekend stay with the Michaelsons. He has a 3:00 PM flight back to Toronto and must leave time for the drive into Ottawa and the traffic along Bronson to the airport.

"I told them," Angie says, "I'm not available today."

Grant watches the rain beating against the big windows that face out from the Michaelsons' kitchen onto their backyard and then down Culpepper Ravine. The water pours off the red shingle roof of the playhouse Eric built for Murielle when she was seven. It runs down the goal posts Eric pounded into the ground when Matthew was a budding soccer star. The late spring earth of Angie's flower garden is mud.

Grant is finishing up his semi-annual trip to Eastern Ontario. Spring and autumn, he flies in from Toronto, takes a room at the Chateau Laurier and spends the week playing client golf at Royal Ottawa or Hunt Club. When the last IT rep or public works bureaucrat has toddled off after drinks and supper on Friday evening, he heads home on the 417 East to Castor. Or he used to head home. Now, he goes to the Michaelsons' empty-nest guest room. He and his sister sold their late parents' house the previous summer, and settled the proceeds neutrally.

Angie is back in front of the stove, facing the dishes in the sink. Grant, expecting she and Eric would be at work this morning, planned a final round at Casselview, the course where he caddied as a kid. The rain changes everything. So, more ambiguously, might Angie's decision to stay home.

"Can't golf," Grant says, "might as well work the phone."

"You're welcome," Angie says, "to use his office downstairs."

"I don't want," Grant says, "to bore you with a salesman's conversation."

Angie starts the dishes, looming over the sink in the way of women shy of their height. She and Eric stayed up after Grant went to bed on Sunday night. Falling asleep, he heard the rain start against the windows. Awakening after midnight, he heard the rain again and then Angie and Eric. He could not tell if they were in the hallway outside his door or downstairs in the living room. Their voices were paired defensive struggles.

"I used to love to dance," Angie says. "Before I met him, I always used to go out dancing. I would go out with Christina and we would just go to places in Kingston and dance. I haven't done that since I married him."

She has a conversational habit of jumping subjects so quickly that what she means gets tangled in what she is suddenly talking about. What sticks out is her new habit of avoiding Eric's name.

"It changes a lot," Grant says. "Marriage."

"Everything," Angie says. "But that you know."

He knows this is not a dig, much less a cruelty. It's a statement of fact about why he is alone. Grant has never been shy about taking the blame for finding it impossible to adapt to life in either of his marriages. He gets up from the table and carries his dishes over to the sink and takes a tea towel off the stove handle. Angie's hands are up to the wrists in soapsuds and she is looking down at what she is doing. Without turning to Grant, she says it's all right, that there are only a few and she will do them if he needs to go downstairs to work.

"Sometimes it's easier," she says, scrubbing the inside of a coffee mug with the bleached-white washrag, "to do things yourself."

Grant notices her bathrobe gaping again. He smells the scent that permeated the sheets and pillowcases in the guest bedroom the night before when he thought the Michaelsons had gone to bed, he got up and came downstairs to get a glass of water and, truth be told, look out the kitchen windows across the yard and down the dark of Culpepper Ravine. Angie was at the counter with the kitchen lights off, pouring a glass of wine. Startling her in the darkness, he touched her arm and apologized. He apologizes again now, without repeating the touch.

"You scared the daylights out of me," she says. "I didn't hear you get up. I went acccck… he'll think I'm a drunk."

Grant laughs and says there is no need for her to be shy about needing something to help her sleep. He dries the coffee cups and the butter knives and a blue toast plate and sets them on the counter beside the draining board.

She laughs, too, that off-the-beat laugh of hers, that inner-secret laugh where the punchline is a mystery to everyone but Angie. "I get by," she says, "with a little help from my friends."

He sees anew how age's softness has elongated Angie's face as if to open a second front of vulnerability. She remains, though, desirable.

The dishes are finished.

"Use his computer," she says, "if you need to go online. He won't mind."

Eric has become a pronoun.

Grant hangs up the tea towel and, as he turns, brushes her

69

bathrobe very lightly, but enough to know she felt it. He notices her bare calves and her large feet in the dark-blue felt slippers. At Castor's centenary picnic, Christina was up from Kingston and Grant heard her caution Angie to watch what she was projecting with her posture. It excited him that her warning might involve him. The excitement was there again, waking and overhearing the Michaelsons arguing.

"I just might," Grant says, "take advantage of that offer."

Alone in the downstairs office, he taps on the keyboard of Eric's ancient PC. Grant started his career writing if-then-go BASIC line code for such relics. He is tempted to download his newest software creation onto the museum piece hard drive. It's a total disk recovery program that has already gained him testimonials from police forces that use it to break up child-porn rings. Vice-presidents of human resources for major Ontario corporations have cited its effectiveness in building cases for employee termination.

Grant could, if he chose, use it to peep into the digital fossil record of his childhood friend's life. Anything Eric has done on his computer over the years, believing it possible for everything to be safely erased, would instantly resurface. He is about to click onto his company's website and tap in his security code when Angie comes downstairs.

She peeps in on Grant. She is out of her bathrobe, wearing black stretch pants and a cotton sweater with broad horizontal stripes of alternating red and white. The pattern emphasizes her breasts, which drift above the laundry basket in her hands. Her hair, pulled back now in a ponytail, remains the same cautious blonde it was when she and Eric married. Her feet are still bare in the blue slippers.

"Will this bother you?" she says. "I'll keep the laundry room door shut."

He goes to the door of the office and watches her walk down the hall. At the laundry room door, she fumbles with the handle. The basket slips askew in her arms and tilts sharply enough to drop one of Eric's black socks and one of her own white blouses onto the base-ment floor. When she bends to scoop them up, her black pants tighten around what Grant can only call her rump, a word he adores more than any other in the English language when applied correctly.

"Here," he says, "let me help."

He opens the door for her and sees her underwear tangle on top of the pile that's already in the laundry room. She dumps Eric's blue and white shirts out of the basket to cover the clump.

"I'm glad I said I wasn't available," she says. "I needed to stay home today."

She bends to sort. Grant goes back to make the last of his calls. Instead of calling, he sits at Eric's desk, in Eric's house, in Eric's absence, and thinks about the Michaelsons being his last connection to Castor.

His mother and father are gone. His sister moved long ago to a former fishing village on Vancouver Island. On Saturday afternoon, in Castor Cemetery, he found his grandfather's gravestone kicked over and smashed ruthlessly to bits. All the possibilities of Grant's childhood – his sister departed, his parents dead, his grandfather obliterated – have come about and now form his past. The past comes to him all-embracing yet empty-handed, like desire without sex, sex without love, love without Heaven, or at least a future. He does not know whether to laugh or cry.

Through the door of the guest room that morning, Grant heard Angie tell Eric she was going to work. Angie is a human resour-ces specialist – a headhunter – who works on a day rate for govern-ment and industry when they need someone to conduct senior execu-tive interviews. She picks and chooses. Eric was coming out of the bathroom after his shower and shave when she lied to him.

When Grant comes upstairs to the kitchen from the base-ment office, Angie is at the table writing something on a yellow legal pad. Her briefcase is open on the chair beside her. She is the picture of someone working from home after all.

"It's funny to be in the house alone with you," she says. "It's like we're the couple."

Could they possibly have been the couple? Eric, fresh from his MBA at Queen's and positioned in the federal bureaucracy, brought Angie back to what was then the new house above Culpepper Ravine. She was a Kingston girl with a Queen's degree herself, though not an MBA. When Grant first met her, she was a pinstriped power dresser. He pegged her as having a future in human herd management.

He was four single malts too deep into a Thanksgiving dinner when he told her she should try launching her own software company in the face of bleeding corporate budgets and the evil of Microsoft if she wanted to know how the world really worked. Neither of them liked the enthusiastic politeness they were forced to use after that.

Then, all those years later, Angie called Grant on his cell. He was in Toronto with clients on the patio at Wish. Eric, she said, had flipped out, took a swing at her without connecting and fled. Murielle had called 9-1-1. Matthew went outside and kicked a soccer ball through the window of his sister's playhouse.

Now, Angie sets her pen diligently down and stretches her arms first upward, then far backward as if reaching through the windows to grasp the rim of Culpepper Ravine. The stripes on her sweater undulate, settle.

"Wouldn't it be better," Grant says, "if couples really were binary?"

"Binary what?" Angie says. "What binary?"

"Simple pairings," Grant says, "of ones and zeros. On and off. Then and now. Or off-on, then-now, at the same time."

"How could life," Angie says, "possibly work like that?"

"Could it possibly," Grant says, "work worse than it does now?"

He laughs. Angie doesn't.

"Sometimes we go for days," she says, "and he won't speak to me. Or he does these kind and amazing things out of nowhere."

"He's been like that," Grant says, "since we were kids."

He is about to heat a cup of the morning's coffee in the micro-wave when Angie gets up to make a fresh pot and they are together in the suddenly small space between the fridge and stove, the kitchen sink, the Christmas gift cappuccino machine. Grant turns from the microwave and Angie is there, too.

"I should go," he says, "up and pack."

In the guest room, he stuffs Sunday's underwear into his bag. He hears Angie come upstairs and is aware of her rummaging around. He is imagining going boldly out and undressing her when she comes in carrying fresh sheets and pillowcases.

"He told me," she says, "about you guys."

The house is quiet around them. It's the kind of sliding, con-scious silence that comes when a song ends at a dance and there's only to choose. Grant looks at his suitcase.

"About us what?" he says.

"When you were kids," Angie says.

"We were kids," Grant says, "thirty years ago."

"More," Angie says, "like forty."

"Forty," Grant says. "I stand corrected. Thank you for that."

They both laugh, but Angie is not about to be redirected by laughter about age. She wants to talk about the past, put it to use.

"In the ravine," she says. "You know."

Castor's landscape is not given to ravines. It forms part of the great slab of Eastern Ontario cornfields, whitewash dairy barns and silver Catholic church spires that separate the Ottawa and St. Law-rence rivers. Flatter, Grant's grandfather used to say, than piss on a plate. Culpepper Ravine's steep rarity made it perfect for exploration, imagination and everything that entails.

73

"We played there," Grant says, "for hours."

"This didn't sound," Angie says, "like playing."

She is in front of Grant, with her back to the door. He steps forward as if to leave the room but stops short. He could reach out and touch her. Touch her arm. Touch her face.

"15 stitches," Angie says. "Or 18?"

"I was stronger than he was," Grant says, "that year."

"The rock to the head," Angie says, "as male equalizer."

"Why," Grant says, "would he tell you about that?"

"We were talking," Angie says, "about you. He said it was important for him to admit what he'd done to you."

"I'm surprised," Grant says, "he remembers. He would."

"He doesn't," Angie says, "let go."

He puts his arms around her waist then, and her arms go around his back and they begin to kiss, a long, very slow kiss and then his mouth slides down her neck and his hands slide lower and stroke. They are working toward it when she breaks them apart. Her face is flushed. She puts one hand on his chest. She is about to say something but says nothing. What could a good wife possibly say when she is on the very edge of fucking the lifelong friend?

She flutters. She calms. She says that all her life she has wanted to be the kind of woman who could just go with the men she wanted to go with, but the way she was raised would never let her be that kind of woman.

"Catholic," Angie says, "and my mother and everything."

"It's up," Grant says, "to you."

"I couldn't," she says, "do this to him. I should after everything he's done to me."

He holds her again but does not kiss her again.

"Simple pairings," he says. "If only."

He lets her go and slides around her to leave the room. She follows him and, at the door, puts her hands around his waist and holds him back and presses her breasts hard against his back. She pulls his shirt out of his pants and laughs her mystery laugh.

"I used to wonder," Angie says, "about you."

"Wonder," Grant says, "what?"

"What," she says, "you're like."

He wonders what her slippers would sound like clumping, one after the other, into the mid-morning rain shadows pooling on the dark hardwood of the guest-room floor. He imagines her long body tensing as he uses his tongue. At some point, he would turn her around and face her away from him, and he would be a dog on a lawn with her, everything but the drool and there might even be some of that.

"We can't," he says, "can we?"

They entertain a last-waltz embrace, everything but the feet plodding around the dance floor in slow circles under the bubbles of spinning silver light, and he begins to laugh uncontrollably. His body pulses against hers from the laughter he can't control, and he buries his face between her neck and shoulder and bites gently into her scented flesh and feels that even if he were to suddenly stop breathing he would not be able to stop this mysterious laughing.

The floor tiles in the Michaelsons' kitchen are bone white, but the afternoon rain light turns them soft grey and makes the long bones of Angie's bare feet stark by contrast. Her body seems to have grown even longer against the planes of the tabletop, the counter, the wall shelf lined with flat stones painted Grade 2 pink and blue and orange. She turns from looking out the window and asks if he remembers what started the fight in Culpepper Ravine. She can't let go, either.

"He was making fun," Grant says.

"Of?" Angie says.

"Me," Grant says.

"For?"

"I told him I was starting a business."

"What's funny about that?"

"My sister told him my business was finding golf balls along the fence at Casselview and selling them back to the grouchy old pricks that lost them. Eric said that wasn't a business, it was scrounging."

"Who," Angie says, "swung first?"

"Who knows," Grant says. "When you're knocked senseless, you don't really remember the before and after."

"He could," Angie says, "have killed you."

Grant wonders, as he does from time to time, what it was like being Eric running through the ravine, falling over outcrop granite and sliding through the spring-runoff mud. How and when, on the run, did Eric come up with the credible tale of Grant slipping on a moss-covered stone? He must have arrived at Michaelson's IGA with his story fully formed. His genius was in seeking out not his own father but Grant's dad, who worked as Mr. Michaelson's produce manager. Grant understands his father was so intent on getting to him in Culpepper Ravine that he never questioned Eric's account. As a business owner, he also knows, Mr. Michaelson would have made it his business to find out what really happened.

Grant made Eric's lie durable for his own benefit. He came home from the Children's Hospital with his head wrapped in bandages. The swathing turned him into the drawings of Lazarus that were handed out during Sunday school in the basement of St. Barnabas Church. It gained him the popularity of a curiosity. When Eric walked across the schoolyard and called Grant his best friend, myths for a lifetime were born.

"I don't think," Grant says, "he really meant to hurt me."

Positioned against the big windows, there is something staged about the way Angie looks back at him in the embrace of grey light. It is as if she has seen this scene herself, pictured it while she was looking out across the yard where Eric's handiwork for their children still occupies such pride of place above Culpepper Ravine.

"It would kill him," she says, "to find out how we feel."

Grant says nothing. Who is he to say anything?

"You never thought," she says, "of revenge?"

It is a question he wishes, for both their sakes, she hadn't asked. Any answer means telling lies that will not work. She crosses the kitchen in her bare feet to kiss him and he kisses her back, trying to come as close as he can to imitating the way he kissed her upstairs when the irresistible laughter overwhelmed him. They separate.

"My grandfather," he says, "grew up on a farm where Upshaw Mall is now. He left Castor when he was 15 but came back and raised a son who became a produce manager in a grocery store."

He sees the subject jump spreading confusion across the softening skin of Angie's face so he does not complete the consequence of grandfather to father to son. Angie is still in her home, in her kitchen, at her windows. Grant's suitcase remains unpacked in the guest bedroom. He will miss his flight. He might still be there when Eric returns from work to ask what's going on. Yet whatever happens next, Grant is already watching from the past where possibilities, chosen or unfulfilled, are all like bright graveyard flowers that ceaselessly bloom and close, bloom and close.

The Family Accidental

Before I became an apostle of world peace – truthfully, a diplomat in the Canadian foreign service and a painter written about in *The Toronto Star* for the subversive geometries of his Universalist vision – I screwed the landlady who was the best friend of my mother and the mother of my best friend. She became a sad drunk with unbearable financial problems. I helped her as I knew how.

It was a Tuesday night in April. I lived in her basement and painted during the mornings in an old shed at the back of her property. Afternoons and evenings, I tutored the town's floundering high school students in math and physics. It earned me enough to pay Mrs. Thwaite the rent, buy groceries, look after details. It gave me enough, that is, to be free to paint without drawing down on my bank account, which was fat and which I intended to keep that way for as long as I could.

Two years earlier, I had topped off my bachelor's degree by winning the undergraduate gold medal in the faculty of education. Instead of going directly into a life of teaching, I spent summers planting trees and winters working double shifts as a labourer in northern bush camps. My option was to go into town on my days off from camp and drink the money away or save it. There were no other choices, but even if there had been I would have saved it. I am by nature a saver.

A childhood gift for math introduced me early to the way interest compounds. I have always loved the feeling of things being set in place and then left to bring their own particularities into being. Saved money, wisely invested, does that. So does a thoroughly considered, historically well-timed diplomatic gesture. So does a painting that has been started, executed, finished with the proper balance of creativity and attention to detail.

Despite *The Toronto Star* art critic's typical lazy journalistic frame grab description of my painting, it is never a question of style or school or form or size or subject (non-subject) matter. It is a question of safeguarding details. When the details are nurtured, protected, put right, the resulting painting can be put on a wall, placed on an easel, hung from the ceiling, whatever needs to be done to let it express its process of growth toward what I, in my headier moments, call its revelation. Each time you look at it should be an opportunity for incremental increase, like money in the bank. That's my aesthetic, the one I was confirmed in when I had enough in my account to take time off to live in Mrs. Thwaite's basement and paint in her shed.

While I was planting trees and banking paycheques, Mr. Thwaite sat up in bed at four thirty on a Monday morning in October, asked Mrs. Thwaite why the room was so dark, put the palms of his hands to his temples, fell out of bed and died, probably in mid-air, from an aneurism. His falling body dragged behind it, and shattered, the bedside lamp that was one of a pair the couple had received as a wedding gift twenty-seven years earlier.

Mr. Thwaite was a local real estate developer who became convinced that the purpose of profit was to justify more borrowing. If he had taken up juggling, it would have been to prove his fervent faith that iron will, hard work, and belief in oneself can make all things travel perpetually up.

When she was three drinks past tipsy, Mrs. Thwaite found it impossible to resist re-enacting how "my Gregory" looked putting his palms to his temples, and reproducing the sound of his body, then the bedside lamp, hitting the floor. She would take on the mystified look of someone enacting a ritual to change outcomes.

Her children, including my childhood friend Niall, were already scattered across Canada. Their return for the funeral gave way in the evening to a drunken fistfight in the living room, and one of the brothers threatening to go downstairs to get a Louisville Slugger left, years earlier, behind a bedroom door. I admit it was while helping the older sister, Tisha, sweep up the smashed crockery in the kitchen that I hatched the idea of becoming Mrs. Thwaite's boarder.

I wanted to come back to my hometown to paint and to investigate some childhood traumas. Awkwardly, my mother had decided, without consulting me, to sell the house in which I grew up. I did not want to live by myself, and I could not move into her apartment. It would mean living too intimately with failure.

I wrote to Tisha from the bush camp asking if she would mind suggesting my idea to her mother. On New Year's Day, I moved into the downstairs bedroom where Niall and I had shown each other our wieners when we were five and six years old.

Then came April. When I came into the kitchen after the last of my evening tutoring sessions, Mrs. Thwaite was at the kitchen table. She was not a little tipsy. She was a rye drinker. She had run out of 7Up. Her federal tax bill was in front of her.

"There's no way I can pay this," she said. "I am a widow."

She was in a state of vulnerability that made me feel as though I had walked in on her in her bedroom while she was bending over a dresser drawer choosing underwear. In fact, I had once accidently intruded on Mrs. Thwaite when she was naked.

Hitting puberty, I had been invited to go with the Thwaites to their cottage at Rolf Lake. Mr. Thwaite had not yet finished building the cottage, so we slept in tents: one for the parents and one for the kids. I went into the kids' tent to change into my bathing suit before going down to the beach to watch the others water ski. When I opened the tent flap, Mrs. Thwaite was already inside, drawing a stretchy navy-blue maillot up her heavy thighs toward her pubic thatch and breasts. She was a strapping woman with long, soft, persimmon hair that she usually kept corralled with a single white elastic.

In the tent, she had taken the elastic off and put it around her wrist for safekeeping while she changed. Released, her hair spilled forward around her face as she inclined at a 45 degree angle that caused her breasts to hang forward and sway. She looked up at me calmly and said she would be only a minute. I could tell, having been around drinking adults enough, by the way she took extra care to settle the bathing suit straps into place and adjust her breasts in the sponge support of the cups, that she was somewhat drunk. I could tell, too, that she still thought of me as the neighborhood kid who played with her younger sons, and that she had not twigged to the implications of my age or what my body was doing or why I was forcing myself to remember the smell of my grandmother's breath when I had to kiss her hello in her hospital bed.

At the table in her kitchen, Mrs. Thwaite was bereft. It was, I later grasped, that moment in the aftermath of a death or a departure when the certainty hits that there is no such thing as moving on. Moving on is a myth. There is only carrying on, and it is the antonym of moving on. It is about bearing, every day for the rest of life, the full weight of everything lost. It is living under the static covering that loss drops over everything when it moves in unannounced, uninvited.

Mrs. Thwaite was not only bereft, she was bankrupt. The amount she owed for taxes was hardly overwhelming. It was $4,327.38, a fraction of what I had accrued in my various accounts. Yet she was not exaggerating or playing for tipsy sympathy. She could not pay it.

Mr. Thwaite had dragged much more than his bedside lamp down behind him. A million-dollar life insurance policy is very reassuring, unless its premium has been diverted for years to keep afloat the line of credit backing the mortgages that went underwater when they were borrowed against penny stocks that tanked.

I spent until almost midnight going through household finances with her. Confession: the sensation of picking through the private details of her getting and spending aroused me just as much as being in her bedroom without her knowledge had years earlier. Puberty again. It was easy for me, the skinny neighbourhood ghost-geek, to slip next door unnoticed and go into the Thwaite's house when they were all out at the lake. I would enter her bedroom – Mr. Thwaite became instantly non-existent – and lie on her bed.

I was too shy and frightened to "go Portnoy" on her, as an English major friend of mine at university described the antics in Philip Roth's novel. I just lay, breathing in the scent she had left behind in the room, holding her pillow – I knew which one was hers – and imagining my arms were around her, avoiding the crucifix and the "Madonna and Child" painting on the wall across from the vanity mirror.

On the surface, Mrs. Thwaite was deeply Irish Catholic. There were crucifixes above each doorway in the house. She made Niall and his siblings say the rosary every night until they got old enough to refuse. Every Holy Week, there were dry, curling palm fronds stuck behind the calendar of feast days tacked to the kitchen wall. It was well-known in our neighbourhood that even when the family went camping at Rolf Lake, Mrs. Thwaite made a point of driving to the nearest village to go to Mass on Sunday.

Did I truly believe, lying on her bed holding her pillow, that if I said the right words in the right way, she would toss aside Mr. Thwaite, the Ten Commandments, even Pope John XXIII, and commit adultery with me? What I know is that I took a huge risk by stealing her black wooden brush with the long red strands of hair in its hard white teeth from the vanity table in front of her mirror. As soon as I got home, I felt so guilty that I took the even worse risk of returning the brush the next time the Thwaites were away.

As a child, I had regarded Mrs. Thwaite the same way my

mother held onto being a Baptist in the face of the world's scorn. My mother simply refused to talk about her beliefs outside the perfect circle of believers. Neither could I have entertained doubts about Mrs. Thwaite's beauty, any more than I could have talked aloud about the sensations she caused in me and which I prayed no one would ever know anything about.

After my happenstance voyeurism in the tent, I became a student of the way others felt about her. Men, I learned by eavesdropping on my mother's conversations with her friends, saw Mrs. Thwaite only from clavicles to knees. Women, my mother included, saw her as a series of enviable proportions culminating in the way that persimmon hair framed the perfect shape and balance of her deep green eyes. They watched their husbands around her accordingly. My mother told the ladies she would trust Peggy Thwaite with her life, but unkind as it might sound, she could not say the same for the men who had too many ants in their pants to know what was making them behave in a certain way.

My mother never showed a sign she suspected what I was going through after I hid Mrs. Thwaite's stolen hairbrush in the art box my father had given me for a twelfth birthday present. Nor did she ever know, I don't think, of the weeks I lay awake at night terrified by my recklessness in returning the brush to the vanity table. I was helpless with imagining that one of the Thwaite kids or Mr. Thwaite or Mrs. Thwaite herself found me in the bedroom returning what I'd stolen and, blocking the doorway, asked me what the hell I was doing. Stealing it was one thing. Keeping it, hiding it, was something else. Giving it back unleashed a kind of compounding from which I could not escape.

Thinking about it over the years, I've sometimes suspected the unrelieved increments of take and return, of impulse and contrition, contributed to me giving Mrs. Thwaite the cheque. Other times, I think I mistakenly believed I was in a position where I could, at long last, cleanly get away with something I wanted to do.

In more lucid moments, I verge on acknowledging the horrifying truth my father taught me: that there are no accidents.

I had reached a point, sitting at her kitchen table, where I no longer wanted to talk about the supermarket checkout line of creditors pressing behind her. She was becoming warmly drunk. I was getting aroused. I also genuinely wanted to help her.

Almost knocking her drink glass over with the abruptness of standing up, I went downstairs to my room and found my chequebook. I came back up with a cheque, dated, signed, made out to her, for $4,327.38. She asked me what it was. I placed it on the table between her outstretched arms, next to her drinking glass with the two sips of rye left in it. She asked me what I was doing. Then she looked down and spoke my first name with the dismay of gratitude.

On the long rides home from the bush camps during my one week off every three months, I would stare out the Greyhound bus window at the elements of the landscape until I lapsed into fantasy about arriving to find the neighbourhood in which I grew up devastated by a natural gas explosion, or my mother killed by a truck careering uncontrollably down the hill into town and crashing into the apartment building where she lived. I would shake my head or shudder my shoulders so violently to clear these images that fellow passengers would lean away as if I were an epileptic about to grand mal. What was embarrassing and frustrating and debilitating about those moments was the paradoxical certainty that if any of the events ever did happen, I would be far too far away to stop them. Yet I would somehow be responsible for failing to stop them all the same: I should have planned ahead.

"Please," I said to Mrs. Thwaite. "Let me help."

I thought she might pick up the cheque and set fire to it with one of the burners on the stove. She did not. She showed me her bitterness. What was she going to do? Clean the houses of other people?

Houses "her Gregory" had built and sold to those people before he pissed every nickel away into some unimaginably vast black pit?

She was shuffling debt between four credit cards timed to the collection agency's calls. The monstrous mortgage "her Gregory" had managed to create was like some alien thing chewing holes in her roof, rooting under the floor in her basement.

Mr. Thwaite – the name came from his family's need for German identity reconstruction during the First World War – had been a housing contractor and then a realtor and then a force for civic expansion. He was no mere nail banger or framer in the housing developments germinating in coyote country on the northwestern boundaries of town. He had bankrolled, or convinced his bank to bankroll, those developments, which he gave names such as Eagle Heights, Mulberry Hill Park and Glen Dornach Estates. More importantly, at least to me, his land speculation emerged from a genuine gift for turning wood into beauty.

He was, by trade, a master cabinetmaker whose tables, chairs, hutches, rolltop desks, brought into rooms for their various purposes, had the power to shift, over time, understanding of a room. The room began to exist as the place where Mr. Thwaite's work was contained. I have witnessed guests in a house walk over to a desk Mr. Thwaite had given someone as a Christmas gift and stand there sliding the doors open and closed to feel the impeccable fit.

He suffered for his art. I do not mean figuratively. I mean disfiguratively. The table saw, mitre saw, band saw, chop saw, the planes and chisels, the lathes and awls and all the tools that he once housed in the shed where I painted had taken their toll. The middle and ring fingers of his left hand were cut off at the first knuckle, freeing him, he always joked, to dance with all the ladies at Christmas parties because he could no longer play the piano. His right palm had been gouged so deeply when a chisel slipped that it left thick red ridges of scar tissue. He made an annual Easter joke of pouring tomato juice from an omnipresent Bloody Mary into his hand and claiming it was stigmata. Despite his own wounds and injuries, he encouraged all his sons to build things. The Thwaite boys were known by their first names in our local emergency room.

Remains of Mr. Thwaite's last project flanked the room where Mrs. Thwaite and I sat. He was refinishing the kitchen cabinets the evening before he died. Most of the dishes – those not broken in the post-funeral fist fight – had been stacked on the counter beside the sink beneath the blank, discoloured spaces on the walls where he had removed the old cabinets but had not yet installed the replace-ments. The few cupboards he had finished and installed were exquis-ite examples of practical promise.

I tried to follow suit. I suggested that Mrs. Thwaite take my cheque, not as charity or another loan she could not afford but as an advance on my rent.

"Four thousand dollars?" she said. "How long are you plan-ning to live here?"

"What about," I said, "modelling fees?"

"Modelling fees?"

She was confused, yet with a drinker's sharp sense for some-thing dangerous in whatever has just been said.

"I need people to sit for me. I would pay you for your time."

"Sit?" she said.

"Model," I said.

I made a redundant circle in the air with my hand.

"How?" she said.

"How?"

"How would I look? What would I wear?"

Light, delayed at the outside edge of the universe by her being my mother's best friend and my best friend's mother, dawned.

"Head and shoulders," I said. "Maybe some studies of your hands. I need to work on my hands."

I wonder, sometimes, if that made her think of what Mr. Thwaite's work had done to his hands. She said nothing about it.

"That's all?" she said.

"It's what I was thinking about," I said.

In truth, it wasn't at all what I was thinking about, yet at the same time it very much was. Having seen her naked up close in a confined space, I wanted to capture her with what would be appraising, though still arousable, eyes. Yet I was mature enough to know that painting a nude of her would cause a problem for the artwork itself. In what basement room could it possibly hang? Who besides me would ever see it?

Mrs. Thwaite would never look at it twice. She would want to burn it, like the cheque, perhaps by setting fire to it on the stove. If it could not be displayed, if only I, its creator, could look at it, how could it do its work of accumulation and revelation? What, in other words, would be the point?

"I don't have to decide tonight, do I?" she said.

She put her hands on either side of the cheque and lowered her head as if praying for, or willing, it to arise and be gone. When she looked up, she had the expression of someone who has awoken from a dream to find she really is in a wheelchair. She got up and left the kitchen, checking the burners on the stove before she went out, leaving me alone with the remnants of Mr. Thwaite's project – the unfinished business of her life.

I could hear her moving around in her bedroom, knew she was getting undressed. I tried to calculate the time it would take her to get to the point of unhooking her bra and letting the straps reverse themselves from what I had seen years before, sliding down her shoulders and arms, letting the cups drop away from her breasts. I tried to calculate but because I could not be sure, I lost interest and began studying the scribble of my name on the signature line of the cheque.

An artist should have a strong signature. I do not. It is weak and immature, childish. Handwriting was one the curses of my school life. I looked around Mr. Thwaite's kitchen and wondered what he saw there in the hours before he put his disfigured hands to his temples and launched over the side of the bed.

Mrs. Thwaite went into the bathroom and began filling the sink. I stood in the hallway and heard the clink of night cream jars. She used the same night cream as my mother. I knew even at age eight that the label colour was called periwinkle. I called good night. There was a hanging silence and then she said good night to me through the closed door.

In keeping with its antique aura, the Thwaite house still had old-fashioned skeleton-key locks on every one of the solid mahogany doors Mr. Thwaite had restored with hand-sanding, scrupulous use of wood filler and lustrous resin finishes to bring out the grain. The keys themselves might well have been buried in the fireplace pit in the northwest corner of the backyard near the small metal shed where the garden tools were kept. I never saw any Thwaite lock a door in that house.

Niall had shown me almost 20 years earlier how to kneel silently down and peep at Tisha as she was getting ready to take a bath. I never did peep, but I was tempted to do so with Mrs. Thwaite, just to see her in a surreptitious, rather than accidental, light.

I had actually seen Mrs. Thwaite twice by accidents of timing. I saw her in my mother's kitchen after I came home sick in Grade 6. As I came in through our long, dark, back hallway, Mrs. Thwaite was facing away from me and toward my father, who hung suspended above his chair for an instant and then, when he heard my footsteps, dropped into it with the speed of a drunk being pushed backward and down.

My father was not drunk. My father was not a drunk. My mother was a teetotal Baptist, and, out of respect for her, my father drank on only a few special occasions a year.

89

Neither was Mrs. Thwaite at that time, though she drank too much at a barbecue once and reportedly said out loud that all Baptists belong in the gutter. My mother refused to believe the report, which came from a woman who did not live in our neighbourhood and was a Pentecostal. The truth, my mother said, was that Mrs. Thwaite came over the next day despite a brutal hangover to help take down all the curtains in our house for cleaning.

So, no, my father was not drunk. But the buttons of Mrs. Thwaite's butter-coloured sweater were undone from the waistband of her brown skirt to the white back strap of her bra.

My father must have seen how pale I was, that I was about to retch for what would have been the third time that day, because he told me without my saying anything to go into the bathroom and hang my head over the sink or toilet. Weak, I felt disoriented by being given an order and a choice at the same time. I heard my father and Mrs. Thwaite walking in the hallway outside the bathroom door. She said something to him that I could not make out because her voice seemed to swirl around the cold, white enamel of the sink the way my father's shaving water, white soap and red whiskers, floating together, hung suspended around the drain every morning when I was small.

I thought Mrs. Thwaite might come in and mother me as she did with all the neighbourhood kids when they skinned a knee or bloodied a nose playing around her house with her children. She did not come in. She was gone when my father opened the door.

He put me to bed but came to the doorway of my room frequently and solicitously to ask if I wanted anything, or just to check that I was all right. Twice he came in and put his hand on my forehead to see if I had a fever. The next day I was fine, and it was a full year later before he left my mother and me behind. The use of silence in diplomacy, of space in art, of forbearance in investing, the foundations for these critical skills were born that day at least in part thanks to Mrs. Thwaite and the undone buttons of her buttery sweater.

Then she came downstairs naked. I was in bed in Niall's old room. Pop star posters and adolescent paraphernalia – including the head and torso charcoal study I had done of him at 14 – abounded. The baseball bat was in the corner behind the door. I heard creaking on the stairs and the brushing bump against a hallway wall of a human body making its way forward in the dark.

I turned on one of the bedside lamps and sat up. Mrs. Thwaite was in the frame of the door. The light startled her and she crossed her arms over her breasts, as she had not done that time in the tent. She looked as though she had just realized that her nightgown and dressing gown were still upstairs, lying on the bedroom floor where she had dropped them.

I refused for many years to let myself wonder why she came downstairs to me. I am a painter, not a writer. I bring objects to surface and surface to objects. I have never pretended to be able to dive under subjective surfaces and emerge with explanations. I deal in light, space and what. Why is for God.

Only as I grow old can I accept that the look she gave me there in Niall's childhood room came from the revelation – self-revelation – of what she was capable of doing for relief, out of vengeance and desperation, to bear the shaming incompleteness of carrying on. She wanted to hurt herself more, and I helped.

Sex occurred with Mrs. Thwaite straddling me, facing the opposite bedroom wall so that it was as if I was taking her from behind. Initially, she had taken me face-to-face and I was able to frame her hair, face and shoulders, her childed breasts as she raised and lowered herself, rocking backward and forward. I could smell fresh rye on her breath: a courage drink or two before coming downstairs. When I pressed my hands on her hips and splayed my fingers across her belly, though, she recoiled and asked – truthfully, ordered – me not to touch her there.

I was not experienced in what childbirth can do to a woman's body. All those years before, the surprise of her breasts, the exposure to her red pubic thatch, were superimposed on me, wiping out detail. With her straddling me, I felt the strange slackness of her belly flesh, saw the skin in the single bulb illumination of the bedside lamp as mysteriously and beautifully mottled as first photographs of the surface of the moon. I did find it beautiful. I am not lying.

Mrs. Thwaite could not overcome her own feeling of disfigurement. She turned her back toward me and rocked me hard so that it was the full pressing weight of her torso, hips and thighs, the auditory arousal of her rump slapping my legs, not the visual aphrodisia of her breasts and face, that brought me off, arching higher and pushing deep, deep, deep into what I could not see. What I could see was her broad white back textured with pores and a loose constellation of small cinnamon freckles and moles, the convex-concave tension of her shoulder blades working under the skin, the articulated vertebrae of her neck as her head bent forward to leverage her effort.

Afterwards, she went upstairs. I heard her walking above me into what I calculated was the kitchen. I wondered whether she was naked or dressed when she picked up the cheque.

Listening in the dark, I told myself no harm had been done, all the while thinking of how my mother had taken to referring to the Thwaites as "the Family Accidental" for their habit of walking around with injuries and wounds from one escapade or another.

Just before sleep, I thought of how my father had returned home early from work one afternoon immediately after I got in from school – almost as if he'd been following me at a discreet distance – and came into my bedroom feeling the urgent need to tell me that accidents do not happen, they are caused.

Thank you, Father, for that traumatic piece of introductory wisdom on the ways of the world.

Orange & Peel

Rope went through the plate-glass window at the Poulet Bar-beque in Westmount right after Christmas, and the shard of glass that followed him out the window just missed stabbing him to death, and fuck those cops are dumb.

"So," Rope said, "Christly fucking dumb."

Daryn, though, wanted to talk about the door in the side of his head that let God in. Usually he listened to Rope's stories, which was a good thing because it gave them both something to do. Today, Daryn had to talk about the door. It was staying open longer and he was afraid, really afraid, that if God could get in so could, you know, the Devil.

"I see your ears," Rope said. "Is that what you mean?"

"I mean," Daryn said, "the door. It opens and God comes in."

"That," Rope said, "is fucking impossible. That's what that is."

"Not," Daryn said, "to me."

Rope did not want to reason. It was January. It was Peel Street. It was mid-afternoon. His ass was freezing, and there was a bottle of Grey Goose vodka waiting for them on a shelf at the SAQ on Ste. Catherine. How much longer they'd have to sit on the snow-and-ice sidewalk outside the House of Seagram being ignored before they had enough to buy the Grey Goose, only God knew. And there was no such thing as God. End of argument.

"Then how," Daryn said, "does He get through the door in the side of my head?"

Rope leaned against Seagram's grey limestone wall as though Mr. Samuel Bronfman himself had invited him to sit down and relax. Why an old Montreal Jew in the whisky business would build a building in the middle of Peel Street that looked like a castle for the fucking King of England was beyond Rope's understanding. It would have been nice if the old Montreal Jew who thought he was the King of fucking England had put some kind of roof overhang on his castle to keep the sky from dropping down Rope's neck.

"Christ," he said, "those cops are dumb."

Daryn still wasn't biting. Today it was all God, all the time. Daryn had gone to some fucked-up Bible college in some dip-shit Alberta town. God and his goddamn door tended to come up from time to time. Today was something special.

"I thought," Daryn said, "you're some kind of Catholic. Don't Catholics believe in God?"

"Some do," Rope said. "Some don't. And some did but don't right fucking now."

It was meant to stop the God talk, but warnings weren't much use when Daryn got fidgety. He might sit there all afternoon and into the dark, talking about God and doors and the side of his head. He would get more and more fidgety and something might happen. Who knew what? Rope would have to stay beside him then because he had saved Daryn from the Frenchmen, and Rope's rule was that when you saved someone you stuck with them. All the while, that beautiful Grey Goose would be waiting in the SAQ.

Rope had scoped it that morning. He'd held it in his hands, pressed the heavy glass bottle against his shirt until the clerk came over and asked him in French if he needed some help, which, translated, meant get the fuck out, bum.

If Rope could still remember arithmetic, they needed another fifteen toonies in the upturned Expos cap on the sidewalk in front of them. All afternoon and into the dark. It took a lot of being ignored to drink quality.

Daryn, before Rope pulled him away, drank with the Frenchmen who lived in the alley further down Peel below Ste. Catherine. Rope refused to drink with them, and not just because they were Frenchmen. They were so far gone they drank dépanneur cooking sherry out of brown paper bags. He knew the kind: he drank for a while with an Eskimo woman in Cabot Square, across from the old Montreal Forum. She and some of her Kuujjuak friends broke into an office building one night and guzzled photocopier fluid. At least drinking quality, you didn't go blind.

"Portcullis," Daryn said.

"Fuck you," Rope said, "too."

"No," Daryn said, "that's a portcullis."

"What," Rope said, "is a what?"

"The black thing hanging over the door," Daryn said. "The fence kind of thing with the black chains hanging down."

"'I'm all ears," Rope said.

"It's called a portcullis."

"How," Rope said, "do you know that?"

"I read a book," Daryn said, "about it."

"A whole book about punt-a-cuntises?"

"Portcullises," Daryn said. "It was about doors."

"Who in fuck would write a whole book about doors?"

"It's in," Daryn said, "the Atwater Library. I'll show you next time we're there."

"Next time we're there," Rope said. "Roger that."

Maybe it was from his time drinking with the Frenchmen, maybe it was from Bible college days, maybe it was just from being fucked in the head, but Daryn had a memory that drove Rope crazy. He could remember chapter and verse of what Jesus said to Mary and Joseph while he was wiping his Holy ass, or the exact page on which Tommy fucked Suzie in some book he'd read five years ago. But he had already forgotten the tables-and-chairs explosion when they went into the Atwater Library to get warm the week before Christmas.

Something about the library's tables and chairs made Rope want to pick them up and throw them through the windows. So he did. That led to him calling Carl, the library security guard, the N-word, which would get anyone barred from anywhere even without throwing tables and chairs around. One N-word out loud and no-way-you're-coming-back-here, mister. He and Daryn would never be going back to Atwater to look at a book about doors.

"They put portcullises on castles to keep enemies out," Daryn said. "Sometimes there would be two portcullises to trap enemies in between and throw burning wood down on them."

"At least," Rope said, "you'd be warm."

Rope's theory was that you should never wear a hat because bare headed made you look more miserable, which you were, and increased the pity factor to make the coins drop faster. It was a theory, and it usually worked pretty well in this block of Peel where the restaurants were middle-high-end and people came and went from buildings that looked like fake castles.

Below Ste. Catherine, it was Harvey's hamburgers and Frenchmen shitting in the alley. Above de Maisonneuve, it was all high-roller cokeheads. The restaurant security people didn't just chase you away for going on the patio in summer and throwing tables and chairs out into the street. They took you into the alley behind the red brick Montreal Amateur Athletic Association building and beat the shit out of you.

Rope was getting too old to have the shit beaten out of him. The night after he went through the plate-glass window at the Poulet Barbeque was his fortieth birthday. He was pretty sure he didn't want to be freezing up against the House of Seagram, held together by bandages and stitches from the Royal Victoria emergency ward, on his forty-first.

"That dumb fucking cop," he said, "offered me a ride down-town from the Royal Vic."

Daryn was busy knee watching and didn't answer. Knee watching was a game where you were not allowed to look all the way up at the faces of passersby but could watch only from their knees down to their shoes and then had to guess who they were and what they did based on the pants they were wearing or the colour of their stockings if they were women.

"Cop," Daryn said.

"I just said that," Rope said. "A cop offered me a ride downtown."

"No," Daryn said, "that was a cop that just walked by."

"The camouflage pants," Rope said,

"The camouflage pants," Daryn said.

"You win," Rope said. "You spotted it. I thought it might fool you, but you got it."

"Those cops," Daryn said, "all wear camouflage pants now. Did you see his cuffs? They were all mucked up, like he's been chasing someone through slush."

"Maybe," Rope said, "he was the one chasing me."

"A cop chased you?"

"Up in Westmount. That's what I'm telling you about. You don't listen much, do you?"

Turned upon, Daryn put his hands to his ears, which were turning frostbite white at the tips and on the lobes. He ran his finger-tips along the side of his shaved head as if feeling for the door God used to come and go. He did it quickly, maybe hoping neither Rope nor the Devil would notice.

"Why was he chasing you?"

"I guess," Rope said, "he had nothing better to do."

It was the lead-in that let him get to tell, finally, about boosting the pork chops from the Metro on Sherbrooke at Victoria and the manager grabbing him at the door and him punching the manager in the face just to get him off, and getting turned around and running down into the basement instead of out the door and being chased around the stockroom and cornered down there behind a palette of Heinz baked beans and the cop being called and the cop escorting him up the stairs but not, for some reason, putting handcuffs on inside the store and Rope breaking away in the parking lot before the cop could cuff him.

"So," Rope said, "Christly fucking dumb."

He started to tell about running into the Poulet Barbeque with the pork chops bleeding inside his shirt and sitting down at a table as if to order dinner and the waitress, the old redhead without tits, coming over and looking out through her red bangs at him and actually sniffing at him, which was what set off his trip through the plate-glass window.

"Do you think," Daryn said, "the Devil could get through the door in the side of my head?"

Interrupted, Rope sat in the ass-freezing cold under the Seagram's green coat of arms, bearing the words Integrity, Craftsmanship, Tradition, and stared at the blue and white Harry Rosen men's wear marquee on the far side of Peel Street. His hands were so cold inside the bandages that it felt as if someone was bending his fingers back to the wrists.

A pair of legs blocked Rope's view of the signs in the Harry Rosen window pitching up to 60 per cent off every suit in the store. The legs were in suit pants, expensive suit pants, not 60 per cent knock down Harry Rosen post-Boxing Day sale suit pants. Rope followed the pant legs up to the dark-blue wool dress coat, to the peek of bright silk tie at the throat under the grey cashmere scarf, past the throat and up again to the middle-aged face with the lizard-skin crinkles under the eyes, grey and black curls curling from under the grey and black fur-and-leather hat pulled down to keep the ears warm. The hat, the ears, the face, the suit, *tout le kit*, belonged to the McGill prof who worked in Catholic studies with Rope's dad.

"What in God's name," the McGill prof said, "have you done to yourself now, Robbie?"

Robbie. Robbie Roper: Grade 1, 2, 3. Robbie the Rope: always dragging stray things home. Robert Charles Roper: warrants, court appearances. Rope-on-Dope: needles and spoons. Rope: what God made him tough as. Robbie: forever there somehow.

"I went up to Westmount," Rope said, "to see my family at Christmas. It got kind of fucked up."

"You were," the McGill prof said, "at your dad's?"

"I peeped," Rope said, "in the front window and saw them all around the big tree without me so I walked back down Lonely Street to the Heartbreak Hotel."

The McGill prof laughed.

"You," he said, "and your stories, Robbie."

"I got a million of them," Rope said.

"Your dad," the McGill prof said, "says hello."

"Not," Rope said, "to me."

The McGill prof didn't laugh.

"You've got to start taking care of yourself, Robbie."

"I'm trying," Rope said, "but so far it isn't working out too good."

He reached up a bandaged hand and the McGill prof fumbled with it in a kind of half-arsed but wholehearted handshake. Rope watched him walk away up the steps of the House of Seagram, which wasn't even the House of Seagram anymore. The Bronfman family had long before donated the fake English castle to McGill's alumni society, which, as Rope's dad wrote in the famous letter to the editor in *The Gazette*, might have been Mr. Sam's afterlife revenge for the university's infamous quota on Jews.

"He always," Daryn said, "talks to you."

"As long as he gives us money," Rope said. "He's my dad's friend."

"He gave us eight bucks," Daryn said. "That hat he's wearing is a disguise."

"What," Rope said, "are those dumb fucking cops wearing camouflage pants for? Are they all on the SWAT team now? Has there been a hostage taking I don't know about?"

"Union protest," Daryn said. "They haven't had a collective agreement for two years."

"How," Rope said, "the fuck do you know that?"

"I read it," Daryn said, "in the Gazette."

"You," Rope said, "read the Gazette?"

"I started," Daryn said, "when I was with those French guys. They use it to wipe their asses after they take a shit in the alley. They say that's all it's good for."

"How," Rope said, "would a bunch of fucking Frenchmen know what the Gazette's good for? They can't even read English."

"They don't care," Daryn said, "about the messages."

"Messages?"

"On the front page of the Gazette. The ones He sends me. I told you about them."

"Do you ever use The Gazette to wipe your ass?"

"The ink comes off on your hands. I don't want to get it all over my ass, too."

"Don't," Rope said, "ever interrupt me like that again, okay?"

Daryn's ears went red, making the white frostbite spots stand out even more. Rope knew the burning was actually going on inside Daryn's head, little licks of flame inside the skin of the skull. Particles of airborne ice were frozen to the top of Mount Royal. An avalanche of winter clouds domed Peel Street.

"Legs, legs, legs," Daryn said. "Tell me why that cop offered you a ride. Legs, legs."

"Fucked," Rope said, "if I know. Maybe he figured I couldn't walk properly with my hands all bandaged up."

"He thought you walked on your hands?" Daryn said. "I have to say legs, legs, legs."

"No, he didn't think I walked on my hands," Rope said. "He just offered me a ride."

"And what did you say?"

"I said 'sure.'"

"And what did he say? Legs, legs, legs."

"He says 'where can I drop you?' and I say 'Peel Street.'"

"And what did he say?"

"He says 'what corner?' and I say 'the corner of Orange and Peel.'"

"And what did he say? Legs, legs. Look at those boots."

"He says 'Orange and Peel? Where's Orange and Peel?' and I say 'Try looking in your lunch.'"

"And what did he say?"

Rope looked up at the sky. Icicles had formed on the flagpole that projected horizontally from the Seagram building. Rope could count six of them, some fat, some skinny, all sharp. Sharks' teeth, Death's fingers, God's coffin nails etc. If they broke loose, they would act exactly the way a shard of glass did when it fell from a broken window. They would barely miss Rope and make him feel confused at having been missed. Or they would hit him on the top of his bare head and slice him open and give him the chance to bleed to death. He held up both his bandaged hands.

"Orange," he said. "Peel. Orange peel. Look in your lunch. There's no Orange and Peel. There's no Orange. It was a fucking joke."

"Oh," Daryn said.

"Oh," Rope said.

"Maybe," Daryn said, "he didn't get it."

"He didn't get it. That's the fucking joke. So Christly fucking dumb, those cops."

"Once," Daryn said, "when I was in that alley where those French guys shit, I thought the Devil was coming out of the steam grate. I was afraid he was going to start chasing me."

Icicles. Icicles. Icicles. Come down, come down, come down. Rope thought his bandages looked like the wraps on a boxer's hands before he puts on his gloves. Or after he's taken them off. Roberto Duran getting that ass whupping from the great Sugar Ray. What a beating. *No mas. No mas.*

"There's no," Rope said, "fucking Devil and there's no fucking God and get that straight if you're going to sit with me, okay?"

"Just," Daryn said, "one more thing.

"No more things."

"One more. Are we still breathing?"

"You won't be if you keep this shit up."

"If we're breathing, there must be a God."

"Roger that," Rope said. "And us living like this?"

"This," Daryn said, "is from getting drunk, not from God."

"I thought everything was from God."

"Oxygen."

"Oxygen?"

"Oxygen is everywhere. But we breathe shit air. Say you're in a cave and your own breathing is what's making the air smell like shit. God is the pinhole in the rock that you put your mouth against to keep breathing so you can stay alive."

"Where," Rope said, "do you get this stuff?"

"Nowhere. Legs, legs."

"From the ass-wipe Gazette?"

"No. Legs. Legs."

"From your fucking Bible school?"

"No. Nowhere."

"From the Atwater Library, with big fat nigger Carl breathing down your neck?"

"Don't say the N-word. In my head. Legs legs legs legs."

Daryn began to rock, always the final bad sign.

"Legs, legs, legs," he said. "Red boots."

"Calm down," Rope said. "Okay?"

"Red boots," Daryn said. "He wears red boots. That's him in those red boots."

"That's not even a him," Rope said. "It's a her. Those are women's boots."

"It's him," Daryn said. "He's dressed as a she. Camouflage. That's what I'm trying to tell you."

"It's okay," Rope said, "Just calm down. Okay?"

Orange and Peel and look in your lunch was supposed to be funny. Throwing stolen pork chops at the waitress so blood dripped down the flat-chested front of her burgundy uniform wasn't meant to be funny. Both things came out the same: Rope with his ass frozen on the sidewalk in front of the House of Seagram that wasn't even the House of Seagram anymore. Daryn was standing, his head tilted back, staring up at the coat of arms. Integrity. Craftsmanship. Tradition.

If it started to snow, it might warm up a bit. Warm made icicles melt. Melting made icicles fall. If Rope were in the right place at the right time, he wouldn't need to buy himself that bottle of beautiful Grey Goose after all. But no. It was too stubborn a day for that. It was cold. It was staying cold. Daryn had discovered the window. Rope got up and stood beside him, for all the good it would do. It was the rule.

The window was small and rectangular and black-trimmed and looked like it belonged on the basement of a bungalow in a West Island suburb, not on a dead rich whisky Jew's King of England castle in downtown Montreal. Behind the window was a leftover Christmas display. It was a scene from *The Nutcracker* with the wooden soldier and the paper castle with the small brown door. No punt-a-cuntises or whatever the fuck they were called. Just a brown cardboard make-believe door, slightly open.

"Oh," Rope said, "fuck."

"Close the door," Daryn said. "We have to close the door."

He was stooping a bit and holding his face close to the window and he wasn't listening to anything the real world had to say any more.

"Look," Rope said, "we've got enough to get that bottle."

He tipped some toonies out of the Expos hat and balanced them on the bandage wrapped around his right hand. The pain, when Daryn knocked his hand away, scattering the coins across the Peel Street snow, almost took Rope's breath away. Daryn's arms began to windmill and his voice became a windup-toy monotone.

"He's getting in," Daryn said. "Close the door close the door close the door."

His fist, when it hit the glass and then recoiled into Rope's face, was a boxer's overhand right smashing nose bone into skull and bursting stars into disbelieving eyes, stars that blew exploding fragments backward into brain moving left to right too slowly to tell the story of what was happening outside, star fragments that became not shards but razor dust mites ripping into the flesh and bone of space itself.

"My eyes," Rope said. "My fucking eyes."

Knocked to his knees, he was talking to Peel Street, or at least to the ice and snow that covered its sidewalk. When he went through the plate-glass window at the Poulet Barbecue, he took the impact on his hands before going airborne. He landed unhurt except for the sliced off parts of his left thumb and right baby finger. He was able to look up and see the manager who had been chasing him looking out through the shattered window. He even had the presence of mind to duck when the shard of glass fell behind him, and again when the manager threw the package of pork chops out the window at his head.

This, though, was a whole different story. He had gone through a window and now a window had gone through him. He knew he should raise his bandaged hands to his face to staunch the bleeding but could not figure out quite how to do that and maintain balance on his knees. It was odd to be in that particular position, unable to see anything, his eyes full of glass, yet knowing the roaring above him was Daryn crawling up through the hole he had made in the window, trying to crawl in to shut the door on the side of his hallucinating head, on the paper castle inside the imitation castle.

Rope knelt. He felt the brush of coat hems and pant legs against his shoulders as people stepped around him. He smelled his own shit-stink breath coming back from the hole that his blood was melting in the Peel Street ice.

Later, as it was getting dark, the McGill prof who worked with Rope's dad in Catholic studies would come down the steps of the former House of Seagram building and, while pulling his fur-and-leather hat down over his ears, notice the broken window and shattered glass on the sidewalk, the crust of blood on the slush near the curb. He would wonder, feeling suddenly old, what had happened while he was inside and where that Robbie Roper had disappeared to now.

Motel Raphael

Louise the Pigeon-Faced Blind Woman is a fixture in Martin's downtown life. As he does every day, going back to his office after noon Mass at Mary Queen of the World, he reaches the midpoint of the crosswalk on the west side of Ste. Catherine and Peel, then reaches into his coat pocket for coins. He weighs the coins in his hand as he approaches her and drops them, *en passant*, in the sawed-off white bleach jug that serves as her begging bowl. Summer, fall, winter, spring, she sits on the sidewalk yowling into a child's blue plastic recorder. She cannot see but hears the coins falling into the jug and raises her chin, nods her head: acknowledgement and thanks. The mongrel English sheep dog that nestles against her leg is less impressed. It looks up dubiously, as though Martin could have given at least a little bit more.

"Hey, pup," he says as an offering, and steps past the corner before he can be identified as the local schmatta mogul who talks to the mutts of street characters.

Recognition makes him anxious. He has a tall man's dislike of being singled out. He accepted, as a mark of arrival, being lionized in *Les Affaires* for his entrepreneurial adroitness. He considered it the price of being an English-speaking Montrealer when *The Gazette* followed up with a feature on him a month later and got most of the facts wrong. Still, he squirmed over his morning coffee each time the stories contained paragraphs about his noteworthy donations to the Old Brewery Mission, Dans La Rue and other urban causes. His wife noticed him holding his breath as he waited for the references to his faith that, fortunately, never came.

Martin's businesses grow fat from the markups on men's golf wear and women's yoga fashions, among other essentials. He knows the risk of becoming one of those remnant caricature charitable Catholics who buy indulgences against the surplus indignities of the poor. Louise the Pigeon-Faced Blind Woman cannot see. Martin does not wish to be seen doing what he has been taught to do invisibly.

"Martin. Here. I'm here."

He looks up Peel against the peat humidity of the late-spring day and sees Huguette. She is standing half a block away calling to him, her long arm reaching high as if to pick something off the roof of the old Seagram Building. The bright pink of her waving palm and fluttering fingers attract and compel. Behind him, he hears the yowl of Louise's recorder. Around him he hears the rutting grunt of a backhoe uprooting pavement, the hectoring of car horns, the Doppler shift of conversations hissing on the terrasses of cafés. He is meeting Huguette in the heart of downtown for the first time. There is always the chance of misunderstanding.

He watches her come down from above him, walking with her delta-water muscularity. Trained as a dancer, now an associate professor of kinesiology at McGill, she keeps her body in astonishing shape. Yet it is her white hair – white colour, white texture – framing the darkness of her African-Indian face that makes all the men who pass think what their sidelong glances show. He smiles – even he would acknowledge smugly – to all of Peel Street. There is no risk. They are meeting only for lunch. And she is his friend. His friend from childhood. What wrong could come?

"Café Saffron is full," she says when they meet. "Did you forget?"

He did. It was his job to make the reservation. Terrasse season in Montreal means restaurants and cafés fill from the outside in. Those who fail to reserve a table on the sidewalk in the sunshine must sit indoors, disappointed before the meal is even ordered. Those who fail to reserve at all must stand in the doorway until they cannot endure being ignored, then slink away.

Huguette does not wait. Neither does she slink. She offers him a double-cheek air kiss to show no harm is done, though he senses he will pay instalments of gratitude for her quick forgiveness. She hooks her finger at him.

"This way," she says. "Follow me. I'll fix this."

She leads him back toward de Maisonneuve. He makes sure he walks squarely beside her, not slipping off her shoulder as though they are strangers close by coincidence. He assumes they are going to Cavalli and pictures the heads coming up above the Armani and Dolce and Gabana as he walks in with a tall black woman with white-white hair who is not his wife. No. She is not his wife. She is a friend with whom he has reunited after decades apart. A friend he grew up with and who he is becoming friends with all over again. Their friend-ship is progressing – has already progressed – from reunion coffees at the Second Cup on Guy to a greasy late Sunday brunch at the Green Spot diner on Notre Dame Street, not far from where she lives in St. Henri. Nothing is wrong.

"Here," Huguette says. "They can slip us in here."

She stops at a tall plate-glass window wedged between Poupart the Tobacconist and the Edifice Hermes. The building is so narrow that Martin always wonders when he passes where the builders have put the door. The last time he looked through the plate glass win-dow, the place was a men's clothing store staffed by elongated young women. Two of them were lounging against a glass counter full of Italian silk ties. One of the young women had a yellow tie in her hands and was playfully wrapping it around the wrists of the other clerk, whose hands were pressed against the small of her back. The shift from clothing store to restaurant seems to have happened so abruptly that Martin is prepared to believe the young women and the yellow tie were just figures in a dream. He remembers an intellectual at a Big Ideas seminar he attended in the Laurentians standing at the front of a room and telling the audience that memory and dream belong to the same class of misunderstanding. Martin wrote it down and is reaching an age where he thinks he grasps what was meant.

"We will be up then, or will we be down?"

The waiter who greets them at the door of Le Chevre Blanc is the word solicitude printed in capital letters in pink chalk on a green blackboard. Except that he forgets to speak French first. Huguette smiles as though she may forgo lunch for the chance to eat him alive. She, like Martin, is Western Canadian born. But she, unlike Martin, is a Montrealer by vengeance. She will assert the linguistic right that comes from being raised by a French Canadian mother where no one knew what to say in her language after *bonjour.*

"How could we," she asks in astringent French, "possibly be down?"

There are only six tables wedged together on the postage-stamp main floor. They are occupied by young blondes nearly identical to those who lounged on the glass counter case in the clothing store. Martin cannot resist glancing at the hands lifting forks to mouths, tilting glasses of wine to lips, to see if there are telltale red circles in the white flesh of the wrists.

"Then we are up," the waiter says.

He switches deftly to French, but Huguette wins on his cowlick of an English accent. Even on an old anglo street such as Peel, engagement in Montreal is won or lost by the perfected shape of a vowel, the correct weight of a consonant. She switches between French and English to make the waiter perform.

"Whatever is most convenient for you," she says. "Whatever you have on the top floor will be fine."

He leads them to the back of the restaurant, then takes them with slowing steps up a classic Montreal wrought-iron staircase that circles tightly to a second and then a third floor. Reaching the banquet-hall-sized room is like coming up for air on the surface of a lake except that the light is inverted, so they rise into deepening shadows, creating the sense of an infinity of tables and chairs and place settings and long-stemmed wine glasses. They are the only customers so the waiter seats them at the table nearest the head of the stairs. It's a minor victory of convenience for him, Martin recognizes, having learned from life in Quebec that literal-mindedness is the last recourse of the linguistically defeated.

"Take your time," the waiter says. "Let me know when you are ready."

He breaks the sentence, like a bread stick, into perfect halves of English and French to show Huguette that he can. She leaves the menu closed as if she already knows what she wants, as if she and Martin long ago settled into the ritual of coming to Le Chevre Blanc alone together, just the two of them. She sips her water and when her glass sets down, they hear the retreat of waiter feet down the spiral iron stairs.

"I discovered this place years ago," she says. It's not the top in terms of food, but it's good as a fallback."

The skirmish with the waiter is ritual. She has played it out before, and wanted to show it to Martin. He wonders, though he would never ask directly, if Saffron really was full. It's an uncharitable thought that he has to push away.

"You were always good at showing me something new," he says.

She gets the reference and he is quickly scanned for dubious flirtatiousness. On a Saturday morning in August of 1967, they rode borrowed ponies down a clay trail through the sagebrush and bunch grass benchlands of the BC Interior to the grey-green edge of the Thompson River. Once there, she got off her pony, ignored their shared adolescent shyness and took off her shirt.

"Boys," Huguette says, "never forget, do they?"

Yet it was she who, after all those years, posted their Grade 7 class picture from Wallachin Elementary on Facebook. It showed the two of them standing side by side in the back row in front of the moss-green gymnasium curtain, both standing out for their height even then. Huguette had the added distinction of being the only African-Indian pubescent girl for several thousand square kilometres who spoke French to her mother, Urdu to her father and Oxbridge English to the kids at school. Oxbridge tinges her English still. When they first met at the Second Cup after she posted the picture, it was her pronunciation that took him home. Her voice was deeper, her body was the fulfillment of ancestry and experience. But, eyes closed, he would have known her from the way she spoke. Language, he has read somewhere, creates the brain in its own image.

"My mother always remembered you," Martin says. "She talked about you all the time. You know mothers and childhood."

"Do I?" Huguette says. "I'll never have children and I don't remember having a childhood."

She is at the age when solitude and loneliness oscillate as history. Present independence is modulated as a lifetime of being alone. He saw it in his own mother, who spent her last 35 years life recasting her entire past into the wave of betrayal that hit her at 50. The complication in Huguette's case is that what she says about not having a childhood is true. In classic immigrant-father fashion, she and her siblings were helping out in the family business when the other kids in Wallachin were just outgrowing watching *Chez Hélène* on snowy black and white TV sets. Yet it's not the whole truth.

"I don't have kids, either," Martin says. "I did have a childhood. I shared it with you, Huguette."

He has stepped across the trip line between catch-up, nostalgia and meaning. She smiles at him and her white hair against the shadows becomes a hood pulled around her face to make everything else disappear. Holding his breath has been a habit for as long as he can remember.

"And then I ended up hating you," Huguette says. "So that kind of cancels everything out to zero, doesn't it?"

He is too flummoxed to double-check the relational arithmetic that gets her to zero so quickly. Hate? Martin is one of those men who can no more imagine someone hating him than he can conceive of his own non-existence. Not everyone he meets or does business with is his friend. But hate?

"Hate?" he says. "Hated?"

She withdraws the word by reaching quickly across the table to touch the back of his hand. Her fingers rest long enough to make sure he understands she is apologizing for surprising him, not retreating from her rightful place.

"As a synonym for 'was angry at,'" she says. "Very, very angry. For a long, long time. You left. You weren't supposed to leave."

The waiter is back. He hovers at table's edge, holding up a small notebook to take their orders. Huguette looks at him as though he is a three-legged dog stopping by to mooch. Her peach fingertips brush against the white hair framing her face. His feet have not yet sounded on the top stair she launches into a story about how furious she was about the fiasco of her father's funeral.

In Wallachin Elementary, she and Martin competed in language arts class to see who could write the best stories. She won most often for inventing tales where each sentence gave birth to the next one in a way that was as implausible yet irresistible as a family tree. In Quebec City, where her mother returned with the father in tow after Huguette grew up and moved away from Wallachin, a feud broke out over whether her father should be buried in Catholic ground or in the "cimetière des anglais" reserved for Protestants and others.

"I told my mother, 'it's none of ma tante's business where

your husband is buried. It's what you want.' It isn't even a Protestant cemetery. There are Irish people buried there and Irish people aren't Protestants."

Martin refrains from mentioning Belfast. Irishness is an iridescent detail, the weave of a shirt picked up in a tie. The theme of her tale is what happens when families act like families. The tale-telling itself, Martin recognizes, is a retreat across the conversational tripwire, back to ground that is safer for her anger.

"Families," she says, "can be so disgusting."

He has a mottled mental image of her, one that precedes standing in front of the green curtain in the elementary-school gym, not yet tall but already waiting tables in the Oasis Motel restaurant. The whole family works for the family business. The French-Canadian wife and mother chambermaids, a working verb, then takes a shift in the kitchen after the kids get home from school. The older brother who never speaks in school, almost but not quite as white as the mother, helps the Greyhound bus drivers load bags, sweeps the parking lot. The Oxford-educated father, dark-skinned as Huguette, comes inspecting through the swinging half-doors that separate the living quarters from the registration desk. Huguette fetches Oasis Burgers and Desert Delight club sandwiches for bus passengers on 45-minute rest stops. Some passengers are Americans who speak in the remarkable accents of the Deep South: They mistake busyness for deafness and discuss Huguette as she passes.

"Racists," Huguette says. "That's all they were. My mother's own family and they didn't want her husband buried in their white Catholic cemetery. It had nothing to do with it being the 'cimetière des anglais.' What language do the dead speak?"

Martin wonders where this roundhouse defence of the father comes from. He does not remember her being daddy's girl. He remembers the father as short and fattening and indifferent to everything until the day the Mounties came to arrest him for burning down his own motel and killing two guests in the process. The waiter must return. Lunch is passing. The kitchen will be closing down soon for the afternoon hiatus. Besides, he is a man with other tables to serve.

"And will Madame be having the large salmon tartar or the small?" he asks in exquisitely careful French.

"Madame," Huguette says in English that is itself as deliberate as if she were counting out coins for Louise the Pigeon-Faced Blind Woman, "will be having the one that is served for lunch."

Enough. He is busy. He is a man with a demanding job. He takes Martin's order and is off, down the stairs and bounding back up again as if he knew in advance what they would order and had it warming in the kitchen. Huguette's salmon tartar is a fingerling hiding in the reed bank shallows of the plate. A half hard-boiled egg, skiffs of red pepper, bob nearby.

"That is the lunch?" she says.

"It is what Madame asked for," the waiter says.

"But it is not what Madame expected," Huguette says. "Nor is it what Madame wants."

The waiter becomes a talking mime, querying with Cartesian rationality precisely what it is that Madame wants and simultaneously demonstrating with hand and forehead how completely unreasonable Madame is being. The menu is opened and consulted. An index finger is traced down its promising columns. No. It might as well be written in Cyrillic for all the clarity it offers. The day's specials are recited in detail a second time but with urgency and a caveat added to their culinary charms. The kitchen, in a handy bit of blackmail, is closing soon after all. But again, no. Nothing there. And then, at the precipice of crisis and despair, a breakthrough. What Madame wants, it turns out, is exactly what she has, the salmon tartare but with the addition of some generosity. Not too much generosity. Too much of a good thing is still too much. Just generosity in right measure. Is that possible, notwithstanding the pending closure of the kitchen? Could he do that for her? He could. He can. He will. But he must fly. The kitchen is many steps away and the kitchen, well, Madame must know about the kitchen: a pit of heartless blackmailers.

What Madame wants. Martin wonders where, in the child Huguette, that particular imperious phrase was hidden, though the flair for the dramatic showed itself as long ago as that summer Saturday morning. Beside the river, turning her back, removing her shirt to reveal the crescent moon of bright pink flesh, folding her arms modestly over the beginning buds of breasts, then jumping back onto the borrowed pony and racing off back up the hill, taunting Martin to catch her. Here she is again, showing him something new. At least, something that is new to him. The distinction, he learned while taking a McGill course called Proust for Entrepreneurs, can be a reason for love.

He tries to tell a story of his own, then, about his own mother and father reconciling after all those years, taking up house together again in the bungalow on Sunnyside, the bitterness, like death, pushed away and held at arm's-length for the time that remained. He tries to make it uplifting but botches the emotion and gets bogged down in the coincidence of his parents meeting again at the Vancouver airport, compounding the overdone with the obvious.

"So she was able to forgive him?" Huguette says.

"After a fashion," Martin says. "Yes."

"I don't think forgiveness has anything to do with fashion," Huguette says. "It's more about exhaustion."

Generosity at Le Chevre Blanc appears to be measured by the teaspoon, which is about what has been added to Huguette's lunch tartare. Dark bread brings miniscule portions of cold pink salmon to her lips as she tells the story of a boyfriend she lived with after she came to Montreal to do a degree in dance at Concordia and to search for her mother's French-Canadian roots. She and the boyfriend shared a walkup on Coffee Street so she could walk to her classes at the Loyola campus that winter.

"Lies," she says. "When I think of the lies he used to tell. He would say he had to go out to meet his business partner and I'd say, 'at 10 o'clock at night' and he'd say, 'we have a big meeting tomorrow, we have to pre-plan tonight.' Pre-plan. Why do people say pre-plan anyway? If you're planning, you're planning. There's no 'pre-' about it. There was no planning. There was no meeting. There was no partner. He'd go to the bar and chase other women."

She finally threw him out, his body, his drinking, his skirt chasing, his lies, all as a package. He did not go without a fight. Pleas not to leave him. Promises to tell the truth. She did not give in. Eventually, he straightened out, grew up, held a job for more than six months. He met someone new. He called to say they were living together.

"So," Martin says, "if he was living with her, why was he calling you?"

"Maybe," Huguette says, "for the same reason you called after we met again."

This time, she does laugh but still reaches across the table to touch his hand. She's sorry. She's only joking. She knows he's nothing like that. She really is sorry. Her fingers withdraw, Martin feels sure a neutral observer would agree, slowly.

"Besides," she says, "aren't you some kind of Catholic? I remember your mother always taking you to church. Do you still go?"

"I still go," he says.

"Every week?"

"Pretty much."

He does not use the word "daily" or mention where he was before they met. His faith does not need her attention.

"That bloody priest," Huguette says, "wanted another $400 to bury my father in the Catholic cemetery. Four hundred dollars. Outrageous."

She spares the waiter the labour of having to suggestive sell the crème brûlée.

"No, no espresso, either," she says. "Lunch was lovely. Merci."

He smiles the smile of someone who smiles for a living and begins to clear away the plates. Huguette knows the work by heart and history. Martin remembers her child's hands doing waitress work, and then the press of her long peach-coloured fingertips on his own fingers, withdrawing so slowly.

"I wonder why men do that," she says.

"Men?" Martin says. "Do what?"

"Lie," she says. "Men don't lie to have sex. They have sex so they can lie afterwards. It's the lying that matters to you. Why is that?"

"I could tell you," Martin says, "but I would have to make it up."

"You think it's a joke? I'm asking you seriously."

When they rode the borrowed ponies down to the Thompson River, she led after the point where the clay path through the benchlands turned and narrowed. Her pony was a black and white Pinto named, incongruously, Charlie Brown. Martin watched its rump sashay past the ruined wooden irrigation flumes built by delusional Englishmen who planted apple orchards in the semi-desert around Wallachin, then went off to France to be machine-gunned in the First World War. At the water, shirtless yet fiercely modest, she asked him if he wanted to touch the crescent moon of pink flesh that curved along the inside length of her right shoulder blade. He still remembers noticing as he dismounted how matted the manes of their ponies were, and the accepting sadness in their dark eyes as they stood so still, looking straight ahead into the heat.

His fingertips still cannot believe the softness of the skin under the path he reached up to trace down her back. Abruptly skittish, she rode suddenly off laughing. He watched the square of her back receding toward the vanishing point, then saw her stop and wait. When he finally caught up to her, he did not think to ask how the mark had come to be on her back. It dawns on him, approaching 40 years later, that is exactly what she, in that mad summer of fire and departure, desperately wanted him to do.

"I guess some men lie for the same reason some women never say what's really on their minds," he says. "They don't have the right words."

Huguette sits as though absorbing his words through her skin, her African-Indian skin, in the deep shadows of the room.

"At home," she says, "when you said something, I always knew you were telling the truth. I remember that. Then you left."

Her tone is not summary but prelude.

Dinner follows lunch though not in a downtown restaurant but in her house, which, like Le Chevre Blanc, wanders upward for three stories to a single top-floor room. Huguette bought the place, an old St. Henri tenement on Bourget just off Notre Dame near the Parc Bonheur d'Occasion, at the bottom of the market when political fear was at a peak and Quebec came within a few referendum votes of declaring itself a country. She lives there alone.

During the guest tour of the house, Martin notices the six doors on the second floor are all ajar at exactly the same angle. The rooms behind the doors are the size whole families crammed into for generations. Each contains only single objects: a bare wooden kitchen table painted green, a pair of scuffed brown children's shoes placed side by side in the geographic centre of the hardwood floor, a ruby-coloured vase devoid of flowers, a black-framed yellow-brown photo of a toothless woman's face. At the far end of the top room's emptiness, a girl's heavy, blue CCM bicycle leans against the far wall below the single dormer window as if its rider has left it there to run an errand or fetch a friend.

"People leave things behind," Huguette says. "I save some of them."

The room they return to downstairs is hardly less spare. They sit at a maple table on the only two chairs in the room. The vase on the sill of the mullioned window facing the street has flowers in it, but only because Martin brought them for Huguette. He ducked into the old florist's across from the Green Spot on his way over and picked out the bright autumn bouquet. She accepted the flowers from him with both hands, a charitable gesture for a boyish misjudgment, and placed them on the far side of the room. They are juxtaposed against the black yoga matt that is rolled, bound and attendant against one of the cream coloured walls and the one black and white photograph allowed in the room.

The subject's face is turned away from the camera. The hair is black not white. But the back muscles define the silver droplets of water on the African-Indian skin. The pink crescent moon has waned over the years. It is still all Martin needs to see.

"It's beautiful," he says. "I can only imagine what this place looked like when you bought it."

She has followed his eyes to the picture and is momentarily confused by the shift of his attention to the whole house. She catches up quickly and, as always, leads again.

"There used to be a brothel next door," she says. "People would gather at the windows in the back rooms of this building to watch the priest come up the alley and go in through the basement door – la porte sauvage."

"He wasn't bringing communion," Martin says.

"Maybe he was," Huguette says, "and just stayed on for afters. Totally corrupt. All of them."

"Our fathers art probably not in Heaven," Martin says. "Not all of them, anyway."

"Who knows where they are?" Huguette says. "Mine had a hard time just getting his poor old body put in the earth. Four hundred dollars extra in the priest's pocket. It's outrageous."

She goes into the kitchen for more wine and when the door swings open Martin smells the sweet earthiness of the lamb and white beans cooking in the *cassoulet*. He considers telling Huguette that the $400 probably bought just enough light and heat from Hydro Quebec so the priest's parishioners didn't have to keep their coats on during Mass. *Cassoulet* is a winter dish and they are hardly into fall, but he won't mention that, either. She pours the wine.

"Your back," he says.

"I have secret passages under the floor," she says. "I can come and go without ever being seen by my guests."

"No," he says, laughing. "I meant your back, not you are back. Your back in that picture. I can't stop looking at it."

"You've seen it before. My back, if not that particular picture."

"Not like that. The last time, I was watching you gallop back up the hill on Charlie Brown."

"He wasn't much for galloping. And who calls a black and white horse Charlie Brown?"

"Who plants apple orchards in a semi-desert? Wallachin was crazy from the river water up. I think it was the English in the genes."

"Speak fo' yo'self, white boy," Huguette says. "Ain't none of that in me."

They laugh together. And yet. When she was eight, her diction was so precise that Miss Cryderman would set aside time on Friday afternoons to have Huguette read to the rest of the class so they could learn how to pronounce English words properly. Naturally, the other kids despised her so she walked to and from school, wandered the playground alone, until Martin, Grade 3 entrepreneur of the heart, saw the chance to make himself his first sale. His too-early attempt to suggestive sell hand holding almost scotched the deal. As she sets the black iron pot of *cassoulet* amid the abundance of dark breads, coarse cheeses, cold *boudin*, leafy salads, he touches his fingertips to the inside of her forearm just above the edge of the bright red pillows of her oven mitt. She takes the mitts off, stays his fingers with her own.

"Not young hands," Martin says, "anymore."

"We should be grandparents," Huguette says.

"No kids. No grandkids. Zero from zero equals zero."

"Would your own grandfather touch someone that way if she weren't his wife?"

"Never mind my grandfather. I used to wake up at night fighting off dreams of my father with someone who wasn't his wife. Who wasn't my mother. Maybe that's why I'm not a father. Or a grandfather."

"But you are married," Huguette says. "And still some kind of Catholic, so you say."

"Yes," Martin says. "I am that."

"Yes," Huguette says. "You are."

She serves him the lamb, offers him the basket of breads, more wine. Decades of memory offer, for the moment, nothing to say. They eat the way they ate sitting side by side on the long wooden bench in the small gym at Wallachin Elementary, waiting to finish before asking what the other wanted to do next, watchful of the outside world. When Martin's father closed the service station down to flee to the pulp mill job and the apartment with Miss Cryderman on Tyee Street in Prince George, when Huguette's father had the second cousin from Surrey burn down the Oasis Motel while the family was in Montreal for Expo '67, the outside world showed how little it cared for their watchfulness. It could bully them as it saw fit. By October, he was trying to survive in a new junior high school in Calgary. She was at a window in Wallachin watching the silver of the handcuffs on her father's wrists as he was led out to the Mountie's cruiser.

"That picture," Martin says. "I'd like to see it again."

He does not realize right away that she has no idea what he means. The meal has him sated, fuzzy, dreamy. It has taken him back to a time when she always knew what he would say before he said it. He is working from yesterday's understanding, meaning that moment in their lives when neither of them would really have been able to say what misunderstanding meant.

"That's good," Huguette says, "because you're looking right at it. Has my cooking blinded you?"

He meant the picture upstairs. The yellow-brown photograph of the toothless woman. He began thinking of it in the silence and now her face is in his head.

"Louise?" Huguette says.

"Louise?" Martin says. "That's not Louise."

"Oh, but it is so Louise," Huguette says. "Louise Lagacé. Louise Éloïse Clotilde Marie-Thérèse Lagacé."

"I thought you meant my Louise."

"I didn't know you had a Louise."

"I don't. Well."

He knows Louise's name only because someone at some point called the cops on her and they came and tried to force her to move from her corner and then someone else called the media on the cops and the media came and brought their short-attention-span illumination to her life. The cops backed off and there was Louise on the CFCF News, secure again in her place, yowling into her recorder, raising and lowering her chin as, by chance, Martin passed by at the moment of clip to drop coins into her sawed-off bucket.

"Look," Huguette says, "you can see the scarring under her eyes if you look very closely."

She'd found the picture in a closet of the room they are standing in. It was in a broken frame, facing the wall. She begins a detective tale of wondering who the woman was and noticing the cat scratch pattern of an old eye injury. By chance, a young man from Concordia doing an oral history project on the black residents of St. Henri interviewed her. He had twin passions for local history and building family trees. He told her about a band of rogue Ursuline nuns who slipped down from Quebec City to Montreal and, without seeking the permission of the bishop, raised the capital and started a school for the blind on Couvent Street. Venture charity. Entrepreneurial love. Huguette was never sure if the young historian made up the part about the rogue Ursulines, but the school existed. At the National Archives, she found her pigeon. Louise was the small girl in the front row in the class picture for 1912.

"The rest of her family," she says, "lived in this room."

Lived until the mother, Lizzie, the brother, Charles, the sisters, Fleury, Béatrice and Huguette, died in the 'flu epidemic of 1918. Louise came back to be with her father. She was nearly 45 when the picture was taken. She did not see 50. Martin wonders what her cry sounded like when the nuns told her that her mother, brother, sisters were gone.

"Her whole life," he says. "One photograph."

"One of her sisters had my name."

"Yes. Coincidentally."

"Coincidentally, it frightens me."

"Frightens? This isn't 1918. You're not going to die from the 'flu."

"It's not the 'flu I'm afraid of. I don't care what I die from. That's just a question of probabilities. Death isn't."

"After my mother's funeral, I calculated she spent 34 years, eight months and some days, hours and minutes bitter, angry, afraid because of the way my father betrayed her," Martin says. "Then they reconciled, and she died first. We all die. Might as well live out God's gifts as best we can."

"We don't all," Huguette says, "die alone. Some of us will. Is that God's gift for us, too?"

Following her back down the stairs, he is thinking about her shoulder crescent moon when it strikes him how odd it is to be looking at her from above. She is tall to his even taller, and he realizes that he always thinks of looking up to see her, looking at a girl's bare back galloping up a hill ahead of him.

History, Martin accepts, has a way of making some things choose themselves. All have sinned and fallen short of the glory of God. Sex occurs in the kitchen as he helps her clear the table, scrape out the *cassoulet* pot, load the dishwasher.

In contrast to the rest of Huguette's house, the kitchen is almost frenzied with objects. Ranks of knives are attentive in wooden blocks along a counter. Silver, brass, iron pans hang from S-swoop hooks along the back wall. Bright spices press together against the glass window of a cupboard door. Baskets contain the spill of walnuts, pecans, almond slivers. Plant tendrils climb over picture frames, windowsills, bowls of fruit.

At one point, she is on the red tiled floor in front of him, facing upward to him but, with her remarkable dancer's body, bending so far backward that her shoulder blades touch her heels. And he is straddling her, she taking him in her mouth, when he has the overwhelming urge to be between her legs. He lowers himself to the floor, begins to open her pants to slide them down. She stops him, both pink hands palm down on his chest.

"Not yet," she says. "Not here."

He scans for alternatives and wonders, in the midst of the euphoria of a swollen cock, where exactly in her house Huguette sleeps.

"The yoga mat?" he says.

She laughs in a burst, touches his face delicately, sweetly.

"Somewhere else," she says. "We have to go somewhere else."

Somewhere else. They have been almost here before. In his early 30s, one of his first franchise stores was in the Cavendish Mall. He was there, visiting Montreal from Calgary to motivate an underperforming sales team. He was standing near the glass counter at the front when he saw her come in and turn her nose up at his blouses, begin her imperious motif with one of the staff. After dinner, he drove her to her walkup near the old Monkland Tavern but then it was he who could not lie to his wife, not even far from home. And here they are again. Somewhere else.

Their coffees are aromatic against their mouths. They sip from travel mugs in the heated leather front seats of Martin's newish car. The warmth is good. They have moved deep into November from the early autumn exhaling of impromptu sex on Huguette's kitchen floor.

It is one of those late autumn nights in Montreal when sudden cold brings the threat of brief snow that no one ever remembers falls at the same time every year because it gives way so quickly to a few days of delusional warmth until winter takes over for good. They are parked in the Secure Storage parking lot halfway down the hill that Montreal slides off roughly at its southwestern edge as it bleeds into its suburbs.

Huguette has brought them here all the way from Summit Circle at the top of Westmount, where they got out and leaned against the stone railing of The Lookout and put their arms around each other's backs and pressed close to look down at the city dying in front of them from the exhaustion of climate and commerce and the breakage of history and the tumours of language. She has guided them here past the dereliction of Picasso's bankrupt restaurant that has been re-opening soon for four years, and the strip of half-hour motels that never close for the night, down to the last slope before the topography flattens out to a flood plain of abandoned trucking yards and cast-off Maersk Line shipping containers and the poverty of Ville St. Pierre and the Autoroute des Souvenirs – the Highway of Remembrance – the escape hatch to the 401, toward Toronto, imperious in its Upper Canadian triumph. Her destination was this particular spot on Boulevard Ste. Anne de Bellevue, across the street from and overlooking the Motel Raphael.

Planning ahead, knowing what she would want, she has brought the coffee in a tall silver flask so they would not have to stop at the Tim Horton's on Cavendish or hit the McDonald's drive-thru before starting down the hill. She offers Martin a refill and he simply nods. Speech will require a bit more recovery. The sex was frantic. Middle-aged citizens with serious reputations to uphold, they went at each other in the darkened parking lot like jailbirds cut loose from prison by an earthquake. Shirt, blouse, bra, pants, underwear, socks, shoes, all were tossed and lost in the car's crevices. Hands and mouths touching feeling holding biting teasing probing tonguing penetrating. Then for Martin, the dopamine dream of ejaculating into the eggless womb of a woman he knew as a child.

Huguette lies back, the electrically warmed leather seat two-thirds reclined, her recovered red blouse an inverted patch of darkness spread across her breasts and belly in a half-hearted gesture of modesty. Moonlight comes in through the sunroof of Martin's car, illuminates Huguette's white hair. Now her hair is a nimbus. Now it is a hood. The steam on the windows seals them inside a cloud. She sips her coffee and looks out the windshield in the direction of the Motel Raphael.

"I lied to you," she says. "Remember that boyfriend I told you I lived with on Coffee Street?"

Coffee Street is just north of them a few blocks, right below Sherbrooke's far west end. They could walk there in a few minutes along the escarpment, past the hooker bars and motels, above the back of the Motel Raphael, if they weren't naked and too drained to look for their clothes.

"Vaguely," Martin says. "He was always running off to pre-plan meetings and you thought he was lying to you? Him?"

"Him. He wasn't a boyfriend."

"No?"

"He was a pimp."

"Oh."

"I met him at a bus stop when I was going to Loyola. He gave me a place to stay. How did I know what was going on? I was a dance student."

"Yes."

"He tried to turn me out in the Motel Raphael. I actually turned up for the trick. Or the date as the other girls called it. I backed out."

"Why?"

"Why did I back out? Or why did I go in the first place?"

Martin has to think. He has recovered enough to recognize there is a sequence to what Huguette says and does. Everything, including the sex, has been a step of some kind.

"Go, I guess," he says. "That's not you. Did you need the money? Did you think you were in love?"

She tells the story, instead, of why she backed out. It was mid-afternoon. She got to the door. It was Room 327. She remembers how empty the room was. There was only the usual motel stuff: the too-bright polyester bedspread, the horrid painting of the cabin with the yellow-orange light showing through the window onto the snow, the matted carpet. She remembers, too, the smell. Under the bathroom disinfectant, the room smelled as if the motel management paid people to sit and smoke in it between rentals. There was nothing, not a thing, belonging to the guy. No suitcase. No bag. No anything. He immediately started negotiating. She immediately reached, as instructed, for the phone to call the pimp to come and get her. The guy handed over the money and dropped his pants.

"He was wearing this red underwear with green things on it that looked like holly leaves. It was like he was wearing Christmas wrapping. And there was his fat pink thing sticking out through the fly."

"You started to laugh?"

"Laugh? What would be funny?"

"I thought you were going to say you started laughing so hard you couldn't go through with it. I don't know. Nervousness. How ridiculous he looked."

"I was horrified. Horrified being there but also because even I knew underwear like that comes from wives who buy it for the kids to give to Dad for that funny kind of love families share at Christmas. How could he even be in that room wearing a Christmas gift?"

She got out of the room. She dropped the money at the door and ran blindly down from the third level of the motel toward the parking lot in ridiculous high-heeled shoes. She twisted her ankle on the stairs, sprawled, managed to get up but couldn't walk. A chambermaid finishing her shift helped her over to the swimming pool and told her to soak the ankle until someone could come to get her. Édouard eventually came and got her and took her back to the apartment on Coffee Street. He told her to wait outside for just a minute while he got the other girls to come down and help her up. He wasn't carrying her up three flights of stairs. When she looked up, he was throwing her things out the window: blouses, skirts, pants, leotards, ballet slippers, black stockings and white stockings, the rain of a bureau drawer full of bras and underwear was coming down on her head.

Plywood covers the windows of Room 327 and every other room in the Motel Raphael. It has been waiting for demolition for years. A Frost fence surrounding the grounds is decorated with signs ordering trespassers not to enter the condemned units. Taggers have climbed over it and strung red-green-yellow-blue gang graffiti around the walls like strands of schizophrenic Christmas lights. Even the sign put up by the company that was going to demolish the motel and build something new is starting to fall apart.

"He kept us there like hostages," Huguette says.

Martin assumes she means Le Pimp Édouard but discovers there is another story buried within the one she has started.

"Three weeks," Huguette says. "Four of us in one room. Like his hostages."

Her father drove them across the country to join Canada's birthday celebration at Expo '67. They got to Montreal. They got to the Motel Raphael. They never got an inch closer to the Expo site. There was something wrong with the car. Buses taking fair goers across Pont Pierre Dupuy to the grounds on the artificial islands of Ste. Helene and Notre Dame were so overcrowded that people were falling out the doors and being injured. The islands themselves, built from the earth excavated for the city's new metro system, were sinking into the St. Lawrence River.

"Lies, lies, lies, one after the other," Huguette says. "My mother knew everything he said was complete bullshit, but what could she do? His hostages. That's what we were."

Martin lowers his seat back until he is almost horizontal. She follows him. Everything below the dashboard is darkness and they are lying together inside it. The windshield is an oblong of moon illumination. They are naked, side by side, staring up through the roof. Dark edges of snow clouds drift into position. Her fingers touch his forearm, stroke his chest, not for arousal now but to make sure he is still there. The stay at the Motel Raphael was all part of burning down the Oasis Motel. If he was in Montreal with his family, he couldn't be blamed for what happened in Wallachin. Or so he thought.

"I didn't think he thought that far ahead," Martin says.

"He wasn't stupid. He had a first in European literature from Oxford."

"I didn't say he was stupid. I always thought it was spontaneous. You know, spontaneous financial combustion. Spur of the moment. Over and done. That kind of thing."

"You don't think he regretted it for the rest of his life?"

She switches sides. She is her father's defender. He got word in the town of Golden at the Alberta-BC border that the bodies of two tourists from Mississippi had been recovered from the ashes. The moronic second cousin from Surrey used too much accelerant for a building that was so dried out by the semi-desert air around it. Fire is always never supposed to spread so fast. The rest of the way home, the family was ordered to be silent, though they did not know why. No one spoke along all the miles of the Trans-Canada through Revelstoke, Sicamous, Salmon Arm, Chase, the highway towns of Martin's distant childhood. At Pritchard, just outside Kamloops, her father stopped the car on the side of the road and got out. Huguette could tell he was weeping, though like the silence, she did not know the cause and was forbidden from asking.

"He knew he was a killer, not just an arsonist," Martin says.

It is the truth without good purpose: cruelty. He is ashamed of himself. Lying on his back beside her, watching the snow clouds form, it occurs to him that the moronic second cousin from Surrey could have bought the cans of gasoline used to burn down the Oasis Motel from only one place in Wallachin. Unless he transported them from the Coast, he would have had to buy them at Ramage's Esso just before it shut down for the night and its owner slipped by to see Miss Cryderman on his way home to his wife. He imagines, now that the last of the dopamine has drained away from his brain, the plan was sealed that night for his father's flight to the pulp mill job and the apartment on Tyee Street in Prince George, Miss Cryderman at hand.

"We've all done things wrong," Huguette says.

"Yes," Martin says, "we have."

"So you're saying what we just did was wrong?"

"I haven't said that."

"So you're saying it wasn't?"

"It was."

"Wrong?"

"Yes."

"Was it a sin?"

131

"No question."

"A mortal sin?"

He takes the taunting. What else can he do? Is he not the one who made the choice to do what he's just done?

"Yes," he says. *"Mea culpa, mea culpa, mea maxima culpa."*

"So how could you do it? Knowing it was a mortal sin? That's not you. It's obviously not about the money. Did you think you were in love?"

She sits up. Where his eyes would otherwise have been drawn to the shifting of her full breasts as she moves, now all he can see is the pink crescent moon vivid again in the spotlight glance of the full moon before it is lost entirely behind the clouds bringing snow. She finds her blouse. Her back disappears.

"You never told me," Martin says, "how that happened. You showed it to me. But you didn't tell me what it was."

"You never asked."

"I'm asking now. Were you burned?"

"Just born," Huguette says. "It was there from birth. Maybe the doctor did something during delivery. Maybe it was genes – some black daddy making some white woman a mommy somewhere in the family long before my black daddy and white mommy had me. I don't know. There are different opinions, different stories."

"You could have told me that," Martin says, "that day."

She is slipping her pants back on but stops, leaving them pulled up just over her knees. An inspecting cop or peeping Tom prowling the parking lot and looking in the window of Martin's car might think what has just been completed is only just beginning. She hovers over him, kisses him so sensuously that he believes it just might be true.

"I wanted to show it to you," she says. "To you."

He joins her in sitting up straight. He searches for his clothes, scanning out through the windshield for inspecting cops coming by to

132

check out why that luxury automobile has been parked in the empty lot of the Secure Storage building for so long. But no. Just oblivious traffic pouring up and down Boulevard Ste. Anne de Bellevue hill. Just cars merging onto Highway 20, heading home to the West Island or godforsaken Laval at the end of the day. Only transport trucks rumbling ceaselessly up and down the elevated ramps of the Autoroute des Souvenirs.

"I should go," Martin says. "I should get home."

"Your wife's waiting," Huguette says.

"No," Martin says. "Yes. Yes, she is."

He finds a sock. His underwear.

"In parts of my father's country," Huguette says, "I would have been judged a goddess or a witch for what's on my back. I would have been worshipped or burned. Come on, Charlie Brown, finish dressing and let's get me home."

Charlie Brown. Apple orchards in a semi-desert. An Oxford graduate holding his own family hostage in the Motel Raphael. Fire and departure. Poor blind Louise. Both of them.

She is a woman who brings a birthday cake to a burglary. She brings it out of its tight and tidy Tupperware container as a surprise after they have finished the wine, eaten the bread and cheese, the cold meats, on the picnic blanket she spread across the concrete floor. Martin provided the tire iron they used to pry the plywood off a back window of the Motel Raphael. Huguette, though, supplied the idea for the break-in and even thought to bring the two sparklers that flare on the top of blue and white cake icing like the retinal scratches of flashbulbs from the 1940s.

"You know I wasn't sure about this," Martin says. "But I have to admit I love it."

They are outlaws in an empty room, break-and-enter artists having their cake and eating it with abandon. Around them, the immediate illumination from the sparklers and the ambient moon-light from their entry window shows everything stripped away await-ing the long-delayed demolition. Wires have been pulled from walls. Walls have been pulled apart. Insulation has been pulled out, forcing them to keep their coats on against the clotted January cold. Fixtures, furniture, pictures, everything but memory is gone.

"A toast," Huguette says. "To making it past 50."

Their wine glasses clink. The sparklers die and she switches on the flashlight. In its conical beam, she slips an envelope out of the seemingly bottomless backpack and slides it across the blanket to him. He licks the remaining icing off his thumbs. It is a pure white card of thick, beautiful coated stock. Inside, there are three lines of elegant handwriting in black ink.

For remembering
Love,
Huguette

The gift follows. It is an oblong box wrapped in dark-grey paper with a single white ribbon and bow. The object inside is crafted ebony, and when Martin lifts it out, a pair of hinged picture frames opens in his hands. The left frame shows a small group of dark-haired girls in deep-brown smocks and black stockings seated on a bench in a room filled by time with shadows. They all lift their chins toward the camera as if on cue from the nun in the white habit that stands at the edge of the frame. Only she looks directly into the lens. The children's eyes cannot see the camera that will make them visible to Martin almost a century later.

"Louise," Martin says.

"There she is," Huguette says.

She has copied the photograph from the archives, connected it indelibly to Martin's life, given him her Louise to hold as fact and memory, dream and understanding.

"You," he says. "Huguette, it's you."

In the picture inside the right-hand frame, her long skinny black arm is lifted upright to wave, reaching so high toward the top of the photograph that she might be trying to pull down a cloud, though the sky is a deep, hot, faultless summer blue. Her light skinned brother looks down and away to a mysterious point in the pavement of the parking lot. The mother leans slightly against the rear passenger side panel of the 1963 Meteor they have travelled in from Wallachin to Montreal. Her smile is the anxious look of someone who wants the shutter released so she can get back to her life, her work, her home. The surprise figure in the photo is the father. He is present when he shouldn't be. He has arranged for someone else to take the snapshot, and stands behind his family, already a little dwarfed by Huguette, with the Motel Raphael sign floating on its post bright as a flag off his right shoulder. In the background, the motel gleams a fresh paint gleam as it elongates along three tiers below the escarpment like an oblong birthday cake made entirely of blue and white icing.

Unless you were from Wallachin, or somehow knew the story within the photograph, you would not know it is a souvenir and an alibi in a single frame. Even the father, with his first in European literature from Oxford, thinks it arranges everything. He is clueless as to how quickly and horribly everything will fall apart.

"There's one more I'll have to give you later," Huguette says. "It's not ready yet."

She pulls a Sure Shot digital camera from the backpack and holds it high over their heads at a 45-degree angle. The tiny flash is like an arrow shower. Blotches like blood red fish swim in front of Martin's eyes. He can only imagine what the wash of light will make of Huguette's whitest of white hair. She tries to show him the image in the thumbnail screen on the camera's back but can't get the backlight right. They show only as outlines.

135

"I'll e-mail it to you at work," she says. "No one else needs to see it. We wouldn't want someone asking questions about it."

It's the acceptance of an indignity, but there is no indignation in her voice. He is sure it will come as no surprise to her that tonight, his birthday, has to be goodbye. No more meals. No more house calls. No more sex. He cannot be a man who goes to daily Mass and then conducts a love affair at night with a childhood friend in the front seat of his car. It's not guilt. It's coherence. He is an entrepreneur. The heart of his life is making the right choice. Huguette's life is the alternation of solitude and loneliness. It may seem uncharitable, but he cannot save her from it.

"Do you know why I wanted us to come here?" she says.

He has no idea. He went along, committed to saying good-bye, even though she threatened to bring along a pair of yellow plastic toy handcuffs that she found in the small backyard of the house in St. Henri. She vowed she would make him sit beside her bound and blindfolded until she was ready to let him go. It was a joke. She didn't bring either the handcuffs or the blindfold. He made a show of being relieved but was secretly a little disappointed. What he would look like as a prisoner or a hostage held in a cold, empty room?

She confesses, then, to a second lie. She tells him the true story of her father's death and burial. The burial in the "cimetière des anglais" had nothing to do with race or language. It was about who can be buried in consecrated ground.

"He ate his last meal in this motel," Huguette says. "He told my mother he had some business to do in Montreal. She was nervous about him driving from Quebec City. He was getting old. He had no business here."

No business beyond cooking a steak and some mushrooms on a charcoal grill that he set up in the little bathroom. He drew himself a warm bath and lay in it to fall asleep inhaling carbon monoxide from the charcoal. The dead, it turned out, spoke the universal language of carbon, dust, tasteless, odourless, invisible gas.

She is standing. He is sitting. He wraps his arms around her waist. His hands move upward under her shirt, his fingers tracing the bare skin of her back. He presses his cheek against her thighs.

"Huguette," he says.

He wishes he had more to give.

"Close your eyes," she says. "There's something else."

He waits for her to kiss him one last kiss goodbye. Instead, she goes behind his back, takes his left hand, pulls it back and crosses it over the right at the wrist. She asks him to stay like that until she gives him the signal to open his eyes and hold out his hands. He waits for the next surprise. After a few minutes, she tells him to stand up. She tightens her fingers around his left biceps and helps him rise. He is to keep his eyes closed and wrists crossed.

"We're leaving," she says. "Stay like that as we go."

"I can't climb out a window without my eyes or arms," he says.

"We're going out the front door," she says. "I'll guide you."

He gives her his trust. He has to after all she has given him. He does not know how she gets the door to open so easily, though she has escaped from this motel before. She guides him down the tiers of the Motel Raphael, step by step. They walk in the dark, though with his eyes closed, it's the cold that matters. For a moment, he becomes anxious. His wife is waiting at home. He has to get home. He should open his eyes and free his hands. He could if he wanted to. He doesn't. He plays along just a little bit longer.

"We're at the pool," Huguette says. "Sit down. Put your legs over the edge."

He swings his legs out above the waterless dark that he cannot see. Without being able to see, he knows, intuitively, that the empty pool is full of dirt, dead leaves, litter from the street, snow, gang graffiti, perhaps even items of clothing left behind long ago. He listens to the traffic coming down the boulevard, passing out onto the Autoroute des Souvenirs.

Sitting in the silence, finally, it is his turn to tell a story. He tells Huguette about something he witnessed right after Christmas. He meant to tell her about it earlier but can't remember now why he forgot. Perhaps it got lost in his plan to say goodbye. He keeps his eyes closed, his hands behind his back, but he feels Huguette beside him, listening.

"I'm walking up Peel Street," Martin says. "I see this panhandler in front of the old Seagram's building. Except he isn't panhandling. His cap is kicked over and there are loonies and toonies and quarters scattered all over the ice on the sidewalk. And him, he's kneeling near the curb face down in the snow, blood pouring down. I see it's pouring out of his eyes. There is this other guy – he looks like a street person – he's smashing a window in the Seagram's building. He's pounding the broken window with his fist. He's screaming something I can't even understand. I realize the guy on the ground has shards of glass in his eyes from the broken window. He's kneeling there screaming 'my eyes, my fucking eyes.' Face down above the snow. Blood everywhere. And everything just the sound of them screaming."

"Was this a dream?" Huguette says.

"No, it was real. I was there. I saw it. I'm sure I did."

"It sounds like a dream," Huguette says. "Like the way we tell dreams when we remember them."

"I know," Martin says. "People were just walking by, brushing past him. It was like a dream that way. You know how, in a dream, people are there but not there? You know what I mean, right?"

"Yes," Huguette says, "I know exactly what you mean."

"I went over and tried to help. There was nothing I could do. I got my handkerchief out and tried to stop the blood, but I was worried putting any pressure on might push the glass deeper into his eyes. The screaming. I can still hear it. 'My eyes, my fucking eyes.' And the other guy, just howling, empty howling."

"Did you call 9-1-1?"

"Someone did. The cops came and arrested the guy who'd broken the window. He was wild, totally out of control. He punched one of the cops in the face and bloodied his nose before they got the handcuffs on him. An ambulance took the other guy away. God knows what happened to him."

He feels another moment of panic, then, suddenly wondering where the pictures are that Huguette has given him as a gift. He begins to open his eyes to run back to the room to check, but she puts a hand on his shoulder. She reassures him. She has the food, the wine, the leftover birthday cake, the blanket, the ebony frame, all in the backpack.

"I have everything," she says. "We're fine."

"You keep the pictures," he says. "For now."

It is really time for him to open his eyes, but he doesn't want to. He should go home, and he will. He likes the feel, though, of Huguette pressing quietly against him, her white hair occasionally tickling his cheek. He likes the way their bodies, vessels of childhood, share warmth against the January night. If she were to bring the picnic blanket out and wrap it around them, they could sit there, not even saying a word, until first light. They won't do that, of course. They have to go. But he wants to stay there, invisible to the world, for just another minute. Maybe a little more.

Where The Lions Are

Tiptoes brought Jenny outside again that summer. The word, heard by accident, let her believe she had finally come through the part of her life when she could only be inside. It was the time after the time when all the boys wanted to come inside.

"Just let me come inside," they said.

They kissed her.

They said, "Just let me come inside."

She let a boy into her room at her mother's house in west Point Grey. People said Jenny got herself into trouble by doing that. They didn't mean she got herself pregnant. They knew she wasn't the Virgin Mary. At the same time, they did mean the trouble was of her doing. Someone else was involved, yet it was her fault alone. It was a time of things being what they were and what they weren't at the same time.

Jenny and the boy crossed Main Street to live in a rented green-roofed house on Venables Street, but before long the East End wasn't for him. The house was a dump, there were too many Chinks, what the fuck was he doing east of Main when his friends all lived on southwest Marine Drive?

He was still there in the pictures in the box on the shelf in the hallway cupboard at her mother's house. Other than there, Jenny didn't know where he was. She stayed inside with the baby. Telephone. Television. The radio brought her outside again. An odd phrase:

"tiptoes down the sidelines." Tiptoes.

Her baby girl, Cora, was lying on the bed in the small bedroom of the green-roofed house. Jenny was tickling the bottoms of Cora's feet. Wee-wee-wee all the way home. She turned the radio on just as an announcer told her she was listening to CKNW, official broadcaster of the BC Lions football team.

She reached to change the station, then realized the game was being played at Empire Stadium, only blocks from her house. There were Lions playing almost in her backyard. If she stuck her head outside and listened, she could hear the roar of the football crowd. It was that close.

She imagined a man in a huge helmet running on his toes down a white, painted line. She had seen images of football while the boy sat pinball-oblivious watching games on TV before he disappeared. She never paid attention to the game itself. Then, by accident, from a radio that just happened to be tuned to a particular announcer's voice, tiptoes caught her ear, made her aware of the game, the running men, the crowd so close to her house. She laughed, alone there, holding her laughing baby.

Not that night but another, Jenny let herself go outside. It took some thinking. Some faith. It took times touching the handle of the back door, peering out through the window at the dark porch, discerning a former tenant's abandoned running shoes tipped over on their sides, a shadowed cardboard box in the corner with objects inside that belonged to who-knew-whom. It took times of withdrawing inside to wait for a better time. And then she was outside.

She listened carefully. She thought she heard the Empire Stadium crowd in the near distance, but she couldn't quite be sure. She began sitting outside. First for a few minutes, then longer. She heard her neighbours in their yards, working in their small gardens, talking on their porches. She could smell the thick tangled odours of tomato plants and sunflower stalks and backyard grape vines growing over the fences that enclosed the alley behind her garage.

One Tuesday night in mid-July, after dark, she went down her back-porch steps and stood on her tiptoes under her clothesline in the middle of her yard and raised her arms straight out to the sides for balance. She began to spin, and she spun until she was dizzy. She spun and spun until her toes tired and she collapsed on the cool grass, laughing. She hit her nose hard enough from the collapse that she could taste her own blood in the back of her throat, but she was laughing, joyous there, lying on the dark grass, moonlit. Behind her was the alley. In front of her was the street. She was herself again, outside again, all new again. In due course, she got a dog.

The dog was an Irish Setter that needed to be walked. She walked with it around the block. Around the neighbourhood. She pushed Baby Cora in the stroller down the little hill on Venables, the setter walking beside. She turned at Rupert, stopped at the corner, pausing, waiting, looking up at the blue and white North Shore Mountains on the far side of Burrard Inlet.

There she was outside, but at the same time she was also back inside. She was inside the unbroken embrace of rock and tree and snowcap that gave the mountains their power to make the city stop, hold still, look up, remember boundaries. "Look here," the mountains said, "look at us, and go no further."

At the highest point of the North Shore Mountains were two peaks called The Lions. According to Squamish Indian legend, Jenny learned as a child from her Brownie leader, if you climbed too close to The Lions you would be swallowed up and forced to live inside their stone bellies forever and ever, world without end, amen.

So, she could not go outside the mountains. She could, though, get to the end of her street. She could walk up Rupert. She could walk all the way up to East Hastings to where it intersected Cassiar. She could look on a map and see that east of Cassiar was Boundary and beyond Boundary were suburbs like Burnaby and Coquitlam and Port Coquitlam and Surrey and then the Fraser Valley and all the Fraser Valley towns she'd never visited and didn't know.

West, of course, was Main and long past that west Point Grey and her mother's house, a place she once knew that now was lost and gone. She could go outside only inside the boundaries of Boundary and Main, within the blue and white limits of the mountains.

One August evening, with Baby Cora in the stroller and the setter beside her, Jenny took a seat on a bus bench on East Hastings right across from Empire Stadium. Buses came and went and she tried to catch the eyes of the drivers to signal to them that she wasn't getting on but they stopped anyway, sometimes to let people off, sometimes, it seemed, just because it was their routine.

She sat on the bus bench watching the crowd filing into Empire Stadium, and she heard the anthem being played, and she could see, slightly, slices of the crowd standing, geometries of bright shirts and dark jackets and older men who still wore cream-coloured straw fedoras in public.

She could not see but sensed the players coming onto the field as the volume of the crowd rose and settled, rose and settled. She had brought her portable radio so she could sit on a bus bench across the street from the stadium and hear the announcer describe what was going on inside. She waited to hear "tiptoes" again.

She knew her Lions – she thought of them as hers now – were playing the Toronto Argonauts and the crowd noise told her when to imagine the collisions of the huge men in their helmets, the savannah-yellow jerseys of the Lions twirling and melding with the blue-and-white sweaters of the Argonauts, the stunning, staccato of male physical violence. Baby Cora slept. The setter settled beside the bench.

Jenny looked up at the North Shore Mountains and said their names to herself and made out the shape of Mount Seymour and saw the necklace of lights on the gondola that took visitors to the top of Grouse. She felt the Lions shifting the August weather. She listened to the football crowd roar for their BC Lions. Lions like mountains. Mountains like lions. Lions on tiptoes down the sidelines.

She began to feel as if the mountains were coming to life across Burrard Inlet, rising and settling, roosting birds. A bus pulled into the bus stop and two boys walked past and looked over at her sitting on the bus bench. The one with bushy red hair and a bushy red beard seemed about to say something to her, but the other, who was tall and lean and balanced like a knifepoint on an acrobat's forehead, touched his friend's arm. They passed on without speaking.

On her way home, when she got to the corner of Rupert and Venables, Jenny turned quickly and looked back and up at the mountains. It was a Vancouver evening when sunlight dying through the corridor of Burrard Inlet lit the blue faces of the slopes and made their edges so sharp and clear it seemed they had moved so close they were looming over Jenny, encircling and protecting her with their beauty and power and might. The Lions – her Lions – could swallow her into their stone stomachs if they wanted and she would not mind.

She slowly pushed the stroller back up the little hill to her house and it was almost dark inside and dark outside by the time she got reluctantly in, and she resisted putting on the lights, lifting Baby Cora asleep out of her stroller pushed to the foot of the bed. Falling asleep, Jenny wondered what that boy with the bushy red hair and beard was about to say.

Two years later, November 19 was a Monday. Empire Stadium was empty. The Lions football team had moved to a new domed stadium downtown near False Creek, on the western side of Main. Jenny still sat on the bus bench listening to the games on her radio, though it was as if the voices of the CKNW announcers were reaching her from some distant locale. Sometimes, the boy with the bushy red hair and beard sat listening beside her. Other times, he had other things to do.

Monday morning was cloudy but mild enough for Jenny to take a chance on hanging some of Cora's clothes outside to dry. She was on her back porch pinning toddler T-shirts to the clothesline when the setter attacked inside. It bit Cora on the arm. It bit her on both legs, on the thigh and at the ankle. When Cora cried out, it bit at her head.

Hearing the cry, Jenny ran inside just as the dog was running out and collided with it and touched its muzzle and her hand came away covered with blood. She wondered why someone would sneak into her green-roofed house to leave a rag doll covered with ketchup under her kitchen table.

One of the policemen sealing up the scene found the setter beneath the white Econoline van in Jenny's garage. It crouched under the differential, wagging its tail between the sagged rear tires. The setter squeezed out from underneath the van and walked stiff-legged toward the policeman. When it reached him, it wagged its tail and tried to lick his hand, making some of Cora's blood brush off on his blue nylon City of Vancouver police service jacket.

"The goddamned dog," the constable said, "It's the god-damned dog."

That evening, BCTV News carried supper hour pictures of the outside of a green-roofed house. A reporter stood in front of the house and identified it as a residence in the East End where a dog had attacked and killed a little girl that morning. An image flashed of a white Econoline van where the dog was found hiding.

The next day, the Province newspaper scooped the Sun by running a front-page baptismal picture of Baby Cora. The picture showed a white-gowned baby held in a priest's arms, with a young mother smiling, bravely bewildered, and a man who looked more like a brother than a father already half backing out of the left side of the frame.

Jenny was taken first to the Hastings-Sunrise police annex, where she was asked to try to give a statement. She was then transferred to Vancouver General Hospital where she lay for several hours on a gurney in a hallway, sedated and muscleless. She was to stay there for observation only until she erupted and left an emergency room nurse on short-term disability with a gouged left eye. The nurse, intending to be attentive, thought the young woman might be comforted by getting out of the peasant skirt, plaid shirt and grey wool work socks she'd been lying in for hours.

"We'll get into you a clean gown," the nurse said, standing over the young woman as she lay lolling her head from side to side on the pale-blue pillow.

"Nightgown," Jenny said.

Her words slurred from her sedated lips. It took the nurse several heartbeats to understand what Jenny was saying, though she usually excelled at grasping the coded needs of her patients.

"Sorry, dear," she said, "no one's brought you anything yet."

This, too, baffled the nurse because she knew why the young woman was there and expected a mother, a father, family, friends to be pressing around the gurney, comforting the young woman and signalling each other with horrified looks above her body. But no. No one so far.

"Nightgown," Jenny said.

Her body went rigid then, and she began barking the word from the back of her throat. Her hands became birds' beaks tearing at the cotton of her own blouse, stabbing at her peasant skirt, ripping the fabric, shredding the threads. The nurse, committing an error of human compassion, leaned over to restrain the hands, and the hands, attacking crows, flew up and stabbed at the pulp of the left eye.

The nurse recoiled. Jenny rolled violently, cracking the corner of her own eye on the corner of the gurney, concussing herself when her head hit the cream and red linoleum tiles. She got to her feet and ran screaming, as if she were again running into the house answering Cora's cry.

"Nightgown, nightgown, nightgown," she screamed until two

orderlies cornered her and subdued her and bound her wrists with impromptu handcuffs of surgical tubing.

At that moment, the nightgown of Jenny's vision was in the bottom drawer of a dresser in the basement suite bedroom of the young man with the bushy red hair and beard. He, whose name was William Perell, lived across from the Frog Hollow Community Centre on the other side of Renfrew from Jenny's green-roofed house. She had left the nightgown behind when the two of them reached the stage of leaving things over temporarily. In the months that had passed, she never bothered to reclaim it. He, in return, left his white Econoline van in her garage.

William Perell had noticed Jenny on a bus bench across from Empire Stadium several times before speaking to her. Even the bushy red beard he'd recently added couldn't give him the confidence he needed to speak to a young woman with a dog and a baby carriage. Then he heard the Lions' broadcast coming from her portable radio.

"What's," he said, "the score?"

"I don't know," Jenny said. "I don't listen for that."

Her answer opened the conversational door for him to ask, jokingly, what she did listen for. It opened the way, after a few meetings at the bus bench, for a ride in his van, but just around the neighbourhood, not out to Jericho Beach as he suggested. The setter rode in the back. The baby carriage was wedged between the captain's chairs of William Perell's white Econoline.

Neither of them would have called what they did together in the following months love, but it felt good being in each other's arms. And William Perell liked that Jenny liked football, even if it was only Canadian football, not the real football played in the NFL. He tried to explain to her that the CFL was a second-rate league whose players wouldn't be allowed to carry water buckets in the NFL. She didn't care. She loved the names of the Canadian teams: Stampeders. Blue Bombers. Rough Riders. Tiger Cats.

"I love Argonauts," she said, "but Lions are my best."

In addition to the Econoline van, William Perell had left behind a plaid shirt and grey work socks, a Bic lighter and a Bic razor that he'd brought over one night when he and Jenny planned to shave off his beard just for the fuck of it. When her green-roofed house came on the BCTV supper hour news, William Perell felt as though he were part of the underlay of the picture. He saw his van, derelict in the garage.

He was about to call his friend Derek Camber to say "what the fuck?" when his phone rang and Camber was calling him. They hadn't talked to each other for months yet there they were calling each other at the same time.

"Camber," William Perell said, "turn on BCTV news. You won't believe it."

"I'm watching," Camber said. "Unbelievable."

"The fucking dog," William Perell said. "I'd have killed that fucking dog."

"I told Jenny," Camber said, "it was dangerous. She wouldn't believe me."

Camber's voice carrying Jenny's name was strange news. William Perell knew Camber knew the young woman. He did not expect to hear Camber say her name.

Camber and William Perell had gone to Templeton High School together. Their friendship was sealed when their Grade 11 English teacher called them "Low Life Number 1 and Low Life Number 2" because they refused, one after the other, to read aloud their parts in Macbeth.

That summer, one of Camber's uncles gave them work at his factory in Surrey. They drove out every morning at 6 a.m. to beat the traffic, and though it was a long drive back and forth, it was fun leaving the East End together in Camber's mother's red Toyota. It paid a lot better than shilling at Playland on the PNE grounds.

Evenings and weekends, they made extra money dealing dope to the kids in Rupert Park. They felt rich that summer, and powerful, and talked about going to Hawaii together for Christmas. Instead, Camber bought a black Firebird in November. William Perell ended up buying the Econoline van at a repo auction. One thing led to another over the years.

The last time they'd spoken was in August in front of a PNE midway booth where a guy was sawing through nails demonstrating the sheer cutting power and invincible durability of Kitchen Magic knives. William Perell thought Jenny had been with him that day but couldn't, for the life of him, be sure. "I warned her," Camber said.

"I caught that dog looking at Cora a few times and I said 'watch out.'"

William Perell wondered how Camber had seen such a thing, and more than once. He wanted to ask where in the green-roofed house Camber had been standing or sitting at the time. He wanted to know what had been said, done, immediately before and after Camber warned Jenny.

"If I'd seen a dog acting like that around a little kid, I'd have killed it," William Perell said.

"It was Jen's dog," Camber said. "You can't kill someone else's dog. It's already destroyed anyway."

First Jenny. Now Jen. And here was Camber knowing about the dog. Here was Camber knowing a lot. Knowing everything, it seemed, even Cora's name.

"You have something of Jen's," Camber said. "I have to come over and get it."

"I don't think," William Perell said, "I have anything here."

"Her nightgown," Camber said. "You have her nightgown."

"Nightgown?" William Perell said. "What nightgown?"

He listened to the silence on the other end of the line to see if Camber could hear the lie.

150

"You have it," Camber said. "Her mother asked me to bring it to the hospital for her."

"I don't" William Perell said, "think so."

So Camber had spoken to Jenny's mother. Had he called the house in west Point Grey? Had the mother called him? How had things gone so far, so fast, without William Perell knowing anything?

"Her mom said Jen left it at your place," Camber said. "She went nuts in the hospital asking for it. You still have it, right, Billy?"

Billy. That was Camber's way of proving who was who in their friendship.

"I'll look around," William Perell said.

He looked around his basement suite. His stereo, his shelves of albums, his stained Sally Ann couch. Monday Night Football would soon be on TV. The New York Giants were playing the Washington Redskins at RFK Stadium. Missing from the camera frame would be Howard Cosell wearing his trademark oversized headphones, looking like a hear-no-evil brass monkey.

ABC had dumped Cosell from the Monday Night broadcast for calling a black Redskins' player a "little monkey" the previous season. Cosell said it was accidental, not racist, and William Perell believed him. Things happened in the heat of a broadcast. People hated Cosell for being a loud-mouthed Jew who used big words, though, so thanks to a mistake with two little words, the network stuck the knife in and Cosell was replaced by O.J. Simpson.

The Juice was picked, William Perell was sure, because he was a light-skinned black who was too safe and dull to harm anyone, even by accident. That, William Perell believed, was the way the world worked. Some people could do nothing wrong no matter what. Others could spend years climbing up life's asshole and, for one mistake, get shit out like Wednesday's breakfast.

"We could take it over together," William Perell said, "after the game. Giants and Skins are playing."

Camber didn't answer, signalling the conversation had already gone on too long and maybe that he regretted a lot of things, including driving all the way out to Surrey that summer of Grade 11 and meeting up again at the Kitchen Magic booth on the PNE midway.

"I'm going to come over and get it," Camber said.

William Perell brushed a hand through his bushy red hair and scratched at the bushy beard on his chin. Camber's voice always sounded like someone who knows a door can be opened when everyone else thinks it's locked. William Perell had learned from Camber how dangerous doors could be.

Camber had won a knife fight. It was at a house party the winter after Grade 12. Someone's drunken jock friend from SFU had mouthed Camber off, and Camber just walked away. When the jock followed him, Camber stepped aside inside the kitchen door and the instant the kid was inside the door frame with his arms at his sides, a butcher knife from the kitchen counter appeared as if by magic in Camber's hand. The kid went down face first in his own blood.

When the cops came around asking, nobody had seen anything, partly because the jock was a college kid who had come down from Burnaby Mountain, partly because Camber had only reacted in self-defence. William Perell, though, believed Camber knew exactly where that butcher knife was the second the SFU kid started mouthing off.

"They showed my van," William Perell said, "on TV."

"Just," Camber said, "the front."

"The cops," William Perell said. "found the dog under it."

"Don't go out, Billy," Camber said, "before I get there."

After Camber hung up, William Perell went into his bedroom and opened the dresser drawer. The nightgown was plain white cotton, shapeless as two pillowcases sewn together. He touched it to his face. It was soft as stomach skin, and creased. Jenny had brought it over so she could curl up in it on his Sally Ann sofa to watch Saturday morning cartoons with Baby Cora sleeping between them.

William Perell had left his Econoline van in Jenny's garage for good reason. Parked on the street in front of his Frog Hollow apartment, it made him think, especially in the rain, of a big, square-backed old drunk down on his knees, unable to get up. Transmission shot. Starter motor going. Passenger-side window smashed in by someone who'd stolen the tape deck and kindly ripped the wiring out of the dashboard in the process. Out of sight at Jennifer's, it was at least out of mind, if not memory.

William Perell and Camber were driving around in the Econoline one night when things with Jenny were, for this and that reason, not what they'd been at first. One thing led to another. He and Camber ended up holding a scab face down on a piece of green foam rubber in the back of the van.

Scab face was a Camber word for the fevered hookers who gave five-dollar blow jobs in the alleys around Hastings and Main. This one they took to the top of the Woodward's parkade, and held her down and burned her hair with William Perell's Bic lighter. She was alive when they opened the back door and she leaped screeching out. Sometime later she fell or jumped from the parkade roof. She died. It was in the Sun and on BCTV news. Camber said the worst they could be blamed for was making a mistake because they hadn't planned on her being so stupid that she would jump or fall.

With the van stored in Jenny's garage, William Perell was back to taking the bus everywhere he went, including on this November Monday night with rain pelting down Renfrew so hard it was hard to even see the outlines of the North Shore Mountains.

William Perell did not know what hospital Jenny had been taken to that morning. He had no idea where she was waiting for her nightgown. His plan was to travel west down Hastings across Main and check first at St. Paul's. Jenny had shown him a picture of Baby Cora being baptized and he knew that meant she was some kind of

Catholic. He carried 15 dollars in his wallet and the nightgown rolled up in a brown paper bag tucked under his arm. Camber, he knew, would come looking for him. And he did.

Here came Camber's black Firebird cruising the curb lane, Camber visible behind the wheel, turning his head to look out the passenger-side window. William Perell walked half a block further down Renfrew to hide. He got back to the bus stop in time to see his bus pulling away and Camber making a left at Slocan, meaning he would circle back for a second time and a third if necessary.

Rain ricocheted from the concrete into William Perell's shins. Rainwater tangled in the coils of his red beard, dripped from his hands as he dropped coins in the fare box of the 10 UBC. He sat near the front, on the bench seat that faced into the aisle. When the bus lurched away from the stop, isolated bodies in the other seats were brought forward in unison from the waist. Passengers shuffled themselves like roosting birds, and sat back. The mechanical wheeze down Hastings began, water and sludge sluicing between the ridges of the black rubber matting in the aisle, white-blue transfer tickets and scraps of orange peel sticking to the metal seat legs.

Across Kaslo, down the first steep hill toward Hastings and Main, a scared kid got on and rode for two stops and rang the bell and got off through the side exit and locked eyes with William Perell through the window as the bus pulled away. A teenaged boy and girl got on. They went all the way to the back seats and immediately began to dry hump for all to see.

The bus flashed past East End Billiards and the Como Market and low, two-storey cinder-block false-front make-a-buck mom-and-pop enterprises. It crossed Commercial Drive. A woman came out of the doorway rain at the Sun Wah Market. She boarded and sat down right across the aisle from William Perell, dripping water from her face.

"Red hair," she said. "Raphael."

Her voice was oblivious. William Perell looked out the window past her but saw everything she was. Her pink cloth skirt and tatty, purple cardigan held closed by a single brown bone button were straight from the old linoleum floor of a Franklin Street flophouse. Orange colouring had been knocked out of her hair, which was matted down on the side where she slept with her face to the wall in a hot-plate room. She wore brown rubber boots that had brackets of grey fur at the ankles.

"I got food, Raphael," she said. "From the Chink."

She reached into a shoulder bag that hung at her side like a strangled cat. William Perell watched to see if she would pull out a knife. She held up an orange. The lurch of the bus made the fruit wobble and fall and bounce on the rubber-matted floor. It came to rest against William Perell's feet. He reached down and picked it up, offering it back, but she had forgotten it already. Don't, he knew, speak to her.

"I hate the Chinks," she said. "They come in my room at night to fuck me."

William Perell winced at the words coming from her mouth. Don't, he knew, say a word.

"I tell them," she said, "get the hell out. Stinking Chinks."

The sentences travelled to the back of the bus and looped back again untouched. Everyone, William Perell knew, was working hard to ignore her. She began to swing her head with impossible, neck-cracking ferocity. The bus driver looked in the mirror. William Perell had to get the nightgown to Jennifer. Yet what was happening was catching him just the same.

"Raphael says to let the Chinks fuck me," she said. "He won't fuck me himself. He used to fuck me all the time."

Her voice was an argument in a room next door. William Perell pressed the soft bag with the nightgown inside tightly to his ribs. He could make this stop by getting up and getting off the bus. What made him need to stay and taunt circumstances to see how much might flow to him?

"Raphael," the woman said, "has red hair like you."

"I thought," William Perell said, "I was Raphael."

Mistake. Mistake. Mistake. No wonder he would spend his life as Low Life Number 2. The woman stopped rolling her neck and stared at him. She came to herself for a moment, then floated away again. Water droplets clustered like beaded insects on the scored flesh of her throat. She began to rock her hips.

"Raphael," she said, "has a big cock. Not like your little Chink dick."

Don't, William Perell knew. But it was too late. At the end of their time together, nothing had really aroused William Perell about Jenny's body. She was, like him, Irish freckle-skinned. Having the kid had destroyed her in some ways. Big and saggy would have been okay, or even totally flat-chested, but she was moderate and ordinary, with the right one drooping enough to make it obviously larger than the left and the pink nursed out of the nipples so they looked like purple-brown smudges from a kid's finger-paint box.

Even when he looked at her as she lay sleeping on his bed, he saw only the stretch marks grooved into her belly and thighs. Nothing moved him physically, then, not even remembering the first nights' sweating pure euphoria. Still, he liked being beside her, close to her skin, as much as inside her. He liked watching her put on the night-gown as much as take it off.

"Chink dick," the woman said.

He closed his eyes as if that would make him disappear for her, but she wasn't seeing him anyway. She was talking to phantoms. He had made himself a phantom by speaking to her. It was Camber who burned the scab face with the lighter in the back of the van. It was William Perell, though, who lured her in through the back door.

The woman's hips began rocking harder. She clenched her

teeth and hissed more obscenities about Chinks, about cocks, about Raphael. The strings of words were strands of bile spit through grinding teeth. The pink skirt rode up her hips.

The bus driver watched through the mirror. His round hat and blue jacket made him look official, authoritative, unlike the younger drivers, who adopted a more casual, shop-floor attitude behind the wheel.

"You," the woman whispered, "got a Chink dick chink dick chink dick."

All William Perell had to do was get where he was going. He had only to deliver the nightgown wrapped in the brown paper bag to give Jenny the gift of the thing she needed on the day her child died. Yet he could not take his eyes off the white insides of the woman's thighs.

A UBC girl carrying books got off at Clark. A balding man with long strands of black hair followed her down the steps. The two teenagers at the back were still dry humping. A thin man wearing a pummelled blue ski jacket over a chocolate-brown suit turned his face to the window and kept one hand on his cardboard briefcase.

The woman's rocking hips pulled her torso down so low her skinny breasts brushed the tops of her thighs. Her pink skirt was rolled even higher now up her thighs. Her neck swung in tight, snappish rhythm. She pressed down hard on her pubic bone with the palm of her left hand.

"Chink cock chink dick chink cock chink dick Raphael Raphael Raphael."

The driver braced his arms across the steering wheel of the bus. The woman slid her hips forward and slumped down on the seat as if to reach William Perell across the aisle. Her left hand reached beneath the hem of the pink skirt. She looped an impossibly elastic arm up above her head and grasped the rear of the seat to leverage her hips higher. The hand beneath the skirt was a digging beak.

Up. Up. The hips rising up. The beak digging faster, faster. The kids at the back were locked in on what was happening while staying wrapped around themselves. The man in the chocolate suit was fixed on the flash of storefronts, rooming houses, used-car lots, but missed nothing of what was going on. The driver was flicking glance after glance after glance into the mirror. Faster, faster hand and hips.

William Perell leaned forward toward the woman, his elbows on his knees. His watch had stopped.

"I cut off," he whispered across to her, "Raphael's dick."

Her release was like something mechanical snagged by its own gyrations. The long, elastic arm pulled her up so high she seemed almost to float.

"Jesus Christ."

William Perell was thrown from the seat into the aisle, where he landed flat on his back, concussed on the black rubber mat. The woman's hoisted pink skirt flew across his vision and she disappeared, moaning a mad stream of obscenities.

"Off the bus."

The driver had hit the brakes in the middle of East Hastings. Drivers in blocked cars began honking their horns. The woman curled, gasping, onto her side on the seat where William Perell had just been sitting. The bus driver left his seat and came back to where William Perell lay.

"The cops are called," the driver said. "I saw what you were doing."

He bent down and put his hands under William Perell's shoulders, pushing him to his feet. The woman rolled off the seat onto the floor, got up on her hands and knees, managed to stand up, staggered down the aisle to the side door, then toppled down the steps out the door. William Perell thought he heard the crack of her flesh and bones on the pavement. Through the window, he could see her lying prone with her skirt pulled up around her hips. A native man,

158

slouched against the door of a storefront Chinese Evangelical Church, looked vaguely in her direction. A woman beside him tugged his arm.

"Jesus Christ," William Perell said. "What the fuck?"

"Watch," the driver said, "your language on this bus."

"What the fuck," William Perell said, "have you done? Call a fucking ambulance."

"Off," the driver said, "this bus right now."

The man in the chocolate suit was standing in the aisle. His suit coat hung several inches below his ski jacket. His briefcase gawped where it had been tossed to the floor and knocked open. It held a flattened lunch bag and a scattering of wrinkled papers. The man snapped the clasp shut and scowled at William Perell.

"I did nothing," William Perell said.

"You egged her on," the driver said. "I saw what you were doing."

"I," the man in the chocolate suit said, "am a witness."

You," William Perell said, "were looking out the fucking window."

"Language," the bus driver said. "I saw everything you did."

The teenagers at the back of the bus stayed where they were, watching, squeezing each other, too excited to laugh. A half-dozen oranges rolled from the woman's shoulder bag across the black rubber matting. One nestled against the bag that held Jennifer's nightgown.

"He egged her on," the bus driver told the constable who was bending his head to make the rain deflect off his City of Vancouver police service hat. Ambulance attendants were loading the woman onto a stretcher. An elderly Chinese man and a young Chinese boy came out of the Hastings Laundry and stood looking over the scene. The woman's unconscious face, tilted at a 45-degree angle as she was lifted, made it seem she had known all along how this would turn out on the very edge of Chinatown, that it was all part of God's great plan.

They stood in the cold rain at the rear of the police cruiser in the middle of East Hastings. The dry humping teenagers wandered away. The man in the chocolate suit stood a few feet distant, holding his briefcase like someone who wanted to be needed. His blue ski jacket was soaked through.

"You know her?" the cop said.

"I don't know her," William Perell said.

"You know her name?" the cop asked.

"I don't know anything about her," William Perell said.

"She knew you," the bus driver said. "She knew your name. She was giving him things. You should check his bag for drugs."

"You should move that bus," the cop said.

"I'll have to await," the driver said, "clearance from my supervisor."

He was a man prepared to make a full report. He looked around for his witness, who had pulled his blue ski jacket over his head and was backing a step or two at a time toward the doorway of Best Value Pawn.

"Move the bus," the cop said.

"I'll need someone's authority to activate the out-of-service sign," the driver said.

"Use mine," the cop said. "Be quick."

He smiled the half smile of authority when he turned back to William Perell.

"You do anything to her?"

"I never touched her," William Perell said.

The ambulance doors shut. The woman evaporated except as the leftovers of a story someone somewhere might tell.

"What's in the bag?" the cop asked. "You got drugs in there?"

"It's something," William Perell said, "for a friend."

"Mind if I look?" the cop said.

William Perell disobeyed the law, but never cops. The cop

held the mouth of the bag open as if a gag-shop snake might pop out. He put his hand in and rummaged around. At the bottom of the hill, on the southwest corner of Hastings and Main, junkies scratched themselves in front of the Carnegie Library. The great 19th-Century philanthropist's name was crusted with filth. It was verdigris against the mud-coloured limestone. Moss across the roof overhang dripped water globules onto the junkies, who rubbed their arms and necks and bent forward at their waists, waiting frantically.

"A nightgown?" the cop said.

"My friend's," William Perell said.

"You steal it?" the cop said.

"Steal it?" William Perell said.

"You one of those?" the cop said.

"One of what?" William Perell said.

"Clotheslines," the cop said. "You one of those guys that steals ladies' underwear off clotheslines?"

"It's a nightgown," William Perell said.

"Whose again? Your sister's?"

"A friend's."

"Where does this friend live?"

"3600 block Venables."

"Venables is the other way. You're going the wrong way to take something to a friend on Venables."

"She's in the hospital."

"You don't say. Which hospital?"

"I don't know."

"You don't know."

"I'm trying to find out. Maybe you could call around for me."

"Maybe you can call around for yourself."

"I don't have their numbers up my ass."

"Look in the phone book, smart ass," the cop said. "Visiting hours are over anyway."

"Visiting hours?" William Perell said.

"Visiting hours," the cop said. "You can't visit anyone in a hospital after eight o'clock unless you're a family member. Are you a family member?

"I'm a friend."

"Well, friend," the cop said. "You're too late."

He held up his watch but it was speckled with rainwater and William Perell could not distinguish the hands and did not want to see anything that belonged to the cop anyway. He took back the bag, which was starting to sog apart. He tucked it under his arm like some deflated thing, trying to keep the insides from spilling out.

A man and woman shoved each other around under the awning of the pawn shop. There was no sign of the witness in the chocolate-coloured suit. An American sailor braced himself with one hand on the plate glass window of the Patricia Hotel and vomited until his round white cap fell to his feet. A black-haired hooker in nose-bleed boots came out of the Sunrise Rooms and stood on the corner of Dunlevy.

"You're free," the cop said, "to go."

Free to go where, he did not say. So much for God's great fucking plan.

And there was Camber. Camber in his black Firebird pointed east up Hastings in front of the First United Church where drunks lay on their backs on every step, face upward to the rain. Camber rolled down the driver's side window and called across the street. William Perell turned toward the voice and shifted the featherweight of the brown paper bag in his hands and then tucked it under his arm again so he would not fumble it onto Hastings. He looked up the street for the cop, but the cop and his cruiser were gone. Camber called again. William Perell turned toward his voice.

"Camber," he said. "What the fuck?"

Camber drew him in. Camber did that. William Perell crossed

to the south side of East Hastings and looked in through the open passenger-side window.

"What," Camber said, "are you doing down here soaking wet, Billy?"

The door locks popped open so loudly William Perell jumped and wondered if Camber had noticed. A bald guy passed, wrapped in a blue and white wool blanket. A spastic leaning sideways in a wheelchair rolled down the hill toward the corner. One of the First United drunks managed to sit upright on the steps. It was as bad, William Perell thought, inside as out and as bad outside as in. He got into Camber's car.

"You wouldn't fucking believe," he said, "what happened on the bus."

He tried to tuck the bag further into his armpit to keep it from becoming a topic of conversation. Camber was watching the sidewalk as if he had a bet on whether the spastic in the wheelchair would fall out.

'You're too late, Billy" he said. "Visiting hours end at eight."

"I know," William Perell said. "The cop said."

"Cop?" Camber said.

"Some lunatic went nuts on the bus. The cops were called."

They both looked across the street. It was perfectly natural that Camber would be there waiting for William Perell, would somehow know exactly where and when to show up. But how could a cop, how could his whole cruiser, just disappear?

"Why didn't you wait?" Camber asked. "We could have gone over together. We could have been there in time, Billy."

The voice was the voice Camber would have used on the phone with Jenny's mother. His let-me-help voice. That was the thing with Camber. He could get what he wanted with his voice or his dick. He didn't need knives.

"I wasn't invited," William Perell said.

"You didn't ask," Camber said.

Actually, William Perell remembered, he had asked. But there had been no answer. There was no point in arguing.

"Remember that summer?" he said.

"We made a lot of money," Camber said.

"It was fun driving out there every morning. The smoke we smoked at lunchtime."

"We had to be stoned. Jenny went nuts. She attacked a nurse."

"I'd go nuts if my kid was killed."

"We used to be friends, Billy."

"We aren't anymore?"

"You tell me."

Camber's Firebird was immaculate. He would spend Saturday mornings washing and waxing it, vacuuming the deep black carpet, rubbing leather protector into the seats and dashboard. It was hard to find a place to step in the cab of William Perell's van that didn't have a Big Mac box or a crushed Coke cup or a crumpled pack of Export A's or the sports section from last Thursday's Vancouver Sun.

"Camber, for fuck sake," William Perell said. "I just wanted to do something right."

"It won't redeem you, Billy"

"Redeem? What kind of word is redeem, Camber?"

"It's a word. It won't help you."

"Did I say it would?"

"You hoped it might."

"Why would I hope that?"

"Because you thought I was fucking her now."

"That makes no sense. Are you?"

"Not right now. I'm talking to you right now."

"Smartass. I meant before today. Last week."

"Not last week."

"Come on."

"Not for a while."

"You stopped?"

"We stopped."

"But you're still going over there?"

"I like Jen. I liked the kid."

"Just friends."

"It's a word."

"So you wanted to bring this thing to her as a friend because her kid got killed. And I was bringing it to her because I thought you were fucking her. What does that make me, Camber?"

"A shithead, Billy."

"Low Life Number 2, right?"

"You said it, Billy. Let's just drive over there and leave a note on the bag saying we both brought it, then go have a beer."

"I can't, Camber," William Perell said. "Not with you."

"Why not with me?"

"We did things Camber. Me and her. You and her. You and me."

"Things?"

"You know what things."

"The only thing you should be thinking about is getting rid of your van."

"Rid?"

"Torch it. Tonight. The cops will go back to Jen's tomorrow to look through it, you know."

"Why would they do that?"

"Because they found the fucking dog under it. And because they're looking for a white van in another matter. And, dumb fucks as they are, they're going to make the connection if you leave it sitting in Jen's garage."

"You knew it was in Jenny's garage?"

"She showed it to me. We looked inside. The door was open."

"You were inside my van with Jenny? What did she say?"

The drunk who'd been shoving the woman around under the pawnshop awning had picked up the American sailor's hat and was wearing it as he tried to perform pirouettes in front of the hooker in red boots.

"It's my van, Camber," William Perell said. "I'm going to fix it up and move to Montreal. I've got an uncle there who owns a printing company. He'll give me a job."

"You aren't moving to Montreal," Camber said, "tonight."

"You scare me, Camber."

"I scare you?"

A mistake, Camber called it. The thing was, he believed it. No the thing was, he could get away with believing what happened to the scab face was no different than if the spastic fell out of the wheelchair or the drunk went down on his knees in the rain in front of the prostitute in the midst of a pirouette.

"You know," William Perell said, "what we did."

"What," Camber said, "did we do, Billy?"

"We killed her, Camber."

"No, we did not. We did not kill her."

"Camber, her head was on fire. We put that fucking cigarette lighter on her hair."

"Well, Billy, it was your fucking van. And your fucking cigarette lighter."

So, this was it. This was Camber the knife-fighter leading William Perell through the door.

"My van? You used the cigarette lighter, Camber. Not me."

"That," Camber said, "would be your word against mine."

Howard Cosell was a lawyer before he became a sportscaster. He was a huge star. He was rich, famous and a personal friend of Muhammad Ali, the greatest boxer who ever lived. Yet when the knife went in, he went down without a fight, flailing his arms.

166

"I always wondered," William Perell said, "how many stitches that kid from SFU needed. I heard it was 51, Camber. Do you know?"

"How," Camber said, "would I know?"

"Maybe," William Perell said, "a cop told you. You talked to them for long enough."

Just because William Perell couldn't win didn't mean he wouldn't fight back. Sometimes all fighting back did was make the damage worse. Sometimes making the damage worse was all there was left.

"You're too late again, Billy," Camber said. "No one saw what happened that night."

"That," William Perell said, "would be my word against yours."

Camber put his hands at 10 and 2 on the steering wheel. The bald guy in the blue blanket paraded back up East Hastings. A drunken man sleeping on the top step sat up suddenly, looked around and lay back down. New junkies began to fill the steps of the Carnegie Library. They looked like sparrows shivering on a clothesline, stripped of their feathers by some airborne parasite that came down with the rain.

"You," Camber said, "would rat?"

"Don't you," William Perell said, "threaten me."

"Who's threatening you?" Camber said.

"I'm not scared of you, Camber."

"You just said you were, Billy. You said I scare you."

"I didn't mean physically."

"So I start the car. What are you going to do?"

"You'll find out."

"Before you could fucking move, Billy, you'd be the one who'd find out. Before your hand reached the door handle."

"You're a fucking psycho, Camber."

"I don't care," Camber said, "what names you call me, Billy."

"You'd cut me?"

"Before you could move."

"In the front seat of your own car?"

"You'll find out."

Up and down the hill leading to the corner of Hastings and Main, moved all manner of human wound. Wheelchairs, crutches, legs akimbo to keep bodies from collapsing, torsos stopping to lean for support against the iron grill over the plate-glass window of Saveway Foods, shoulders shaking heading up to the Balmoral Hotel, hands palming 25 cents for a beer, feet scuttering down the steps of the Carnegie Library to get around the corner into the alley to fix.

A drunken woman sitting on the church steps got up, looked up the hill and down, unsure where to go, looking, William Perell was sure, like she was about to suffocate.

"You knife me," William Perell said, "and I'll bleed all over it."

He shifted the nightgown bag diagonally across his chest like the strap of a shield. No matter where Camber's knife slashed or stabbed, the white cotton nightgown would absorb the blood. William Perell almost laughed out loud, realizing he was so weak that he could stay in the fight only by threatening to bleed to death.

And yet it worked. It worked.

Camber shifted his hands slightly on the wheel, not in a threatening way but in the manner of someone positioning himself for a chin-up in a high-school gym.

"Okay, Billy," he said. "You win."

William Perell knew this wasn't even close to being true, but it was his chance to get out. Before Camber could move, William Perell was on the curb, slamming shut the passenger-side door, Jenny's nightgown tucked back under his arm. Camber stayed inside, leaning forward in the immaculate phosphorescent dashboard light, taking out a Bic lighter and pointing it toward the window.

Without the flame igniting, William Perell could almost see the McDonald's cups and cigarette packages and sports sections beginning to curl into flames on the floorboards of his van. He could almost taste the smoke as it burst through the roof of the garage, feel the grit of the soot spreading across the green-roofed house.

So there William Perell was, walking down East Hastings carrying Jenny's nightgown next to his ribs. All those weeks, the nightgown lay in the drawer of his bedroom dresser and now he was just carrying it with him, not knowing where she was and too late to get there anyway. For all that nothing aroused him about her at the end, for all that Camber had won again and would always win each and every time, William Perell had wanted to bring something of Jenny's back. Shapeless and white the nightgown might be, but it had been her second skin. He thought about watching her take it off just so he could watch her put it on.

"Fuck?"

A skin-and-bones scab face with eyes three-quarters closed was propped against the doorway of the East-West Rooms. She was so skinny that a hard wind might blow her around like the paper bags plastered to the front of Dykstra's Pharmacy. He, William Perell, was down with the scab faces again. Life had shit him out like last Wednesday's breakfast.

"You?" he said,

"You," the scab face said. "want to fuck me?"

"No," William Perell said, "fucking way."

"Fuck you," she said, "asshole."

William Perell had some words on his tongue for her but held them. Trouble down here came with a knife. Everyone had Camber's power to make blades magically appear. Every coat sleeve, every waistband, every boot top was dangerous. Don't, he knew, say anything.

"Fuck it," William Perell said. "Just fuck it."

"Just," the scab face said, "fuck off."

She pronounced it "jist" in a wary, spitting way although her lips barely moved. These blocks of East Hastings stunk of gut stink.

169

It was more than the pissing and shitting that went on in the alleys and between the buildings. It was the drunks and the addicts being washed away by the juices in their own guts, the stomach acids that sloshed around with the cooking sherry and the vanilla extract and the Bay Rum and the Lysol taken straight, no chaser, from a hole punched in the side of a can stolen just to make the morning and then the afternoon shakes go away. The scab face's right hand drooped toward her hip.

"I changed my mind," William Perell said. "I do want to fuck."

"Fuck off," she said.

"How," William Perell said, "much?"

Her eyelids, below a lock of beeswax hair, were almost able to move. That was the sign a scab face was hooked. Camber had invented scab face for two girls in their Grade 11 class at Templeton. The girls gave Camber and William Perell blow jobs in return for the bags of dope they needed to get over the zit whites infesting their cheeks and foreheads. Scab faces.

William Perell had watched the two girls cross over to the point where no more flesh could come off the bone, the scarred cheeks couldn't hollow any more, the eyes could not be any more unseeing. All that was left for them was to die huddled behind a dumpster or on the floor of a fleabag room. Scab faces.

From the name to the act, Camber and William Perell would taunt scab faces into the Econoline van for five bucks or less. Sometimes they would drive them out to Jericho Beach and do them and dump them, half-naked and needing to fix, on the streets and doorsteps of rich cocksuckers in west Point Grey. The scab face in front of William Perell now managed something that she probably thought was a smile.

"You want me?" she said. "A hundred bucks."

William Perell wondered if she would die that night. He wondered what sound she would make from those punched-out lips just

170

as she collapsed.

"I've got five bucks," he said. "Take it or leave it."

"Fuck," she said, "you."

"Sure," William Perell said. "For five bucks."

He tightened his arm around the paper bag, out of the scab face's swollen sight.

"Not for a fuck," she said. "I'm not fucking for five. A blow job. Five for a blow job. Twenty for a fuck. Fifteen."

"Five," William Perell said.

The hand that had been on her hip came forward, palm upward, a beggar's empty plea. No knife.

"You got," she said, "a car?"

Both her hands were in the upturned cupped position now. She would go down on her knees soon.

"In the alley," William Perell said. "Back there."

The crawl space between the East-West Rooms and Dykstra's Pharmacy was so narrow that the scab face and William Perell had to walk single file. The only illumination came from the street lights reflecting off a strip of white mist hovering above the rooftops of the two buildings. William Perell ran his fingertips along the stone walls to keep from stumbling in the suffocating gut stink. He was ready to turn and run if anyone blocked either end to trap him inside. If they sealed up both ends against him, he would grab the scab face by the throat and push her forward as a blocker, a shield, threatening to break her neck or strangle her. He just had to hope whoever was there would care.

When they got into the alley, he backed her up so she was wedged between the flophouse wall and the corner of the drug-store's dumpster. The scab face eyes flinched. The movement, under the incongruous hair, showed the horror of her face. She was a little younger, even, than the two girls in his high school class had been. She wore a black miniskirt made from some cheap plastic crap. On her feet were filthy canvas running shoes with frayed holes near the toes. He put his hands on her bone shoulders and forced her to her knees.

"I've only got two bucks," he said.

"Fuck you," she said.

"In," William Perell said, "a minute."

"Let me up," the scab face said. "You fucking let me up."

But there was nothing inside her voice. She would take the two. She would take a dollar. She was hooked, hooked, hooked. And yet she had something, as William Perell imagined they almost always did until they collapsed for good.

"What's," she said, "in that bag?"

"None," William Perell said, "of your fucking business."

She rocked back on her knees to take him into her mouth. She unzipped him and crow's claws reached into his pants to pull his cock out into the wet November Monday night. He let the nightgown slide to the ground beside his left foot. What did he care now about Jenny's nightgown? Too late now. Too late.

"Fuck it," William Perell said.

"Now?" the scab face said.

"Be quick," William Perell said.

"Not up the ass," she said. "Not for two bucks."

"Up anything I want," he said. "You just stand still."

"Fuck you," she said.

But she bent over and raised her wasted rump in the air. William Perell's cock followed her rising. He almost blew off watching her turn, put her palms against the wall, make a sagged saddle of her back. She hitched up her black plastic skirt and spread-eagled upright, her head down between her legs, her right shoulder brushing against the dumpster. Her fluid stink made him gag, but gagging, he walked up behind her and stuck himself into something. He wasn't quite sure which hole. Or why.

Finished, he wiped himself on her skirt and that set her off.

172

Screaming, she turned to swing at him and he dodged and she kicked at the brown paper bag holding Jenny's nightgown, and with a speed that stunned him, she scooped it up and began to run. William Perell tackled her around the waist a few feet into the black space between the flophouse and the drugstore. Both their heads cracked off the facing walls. He felt blood in the back of this throat and couldn't tell if it was his own or the scab face's. Skinny as she was, she twisted powerfully away from him and the bag flounced out and he dove over top of her to grab the bag and run. All he wanted to do at that moment was run. Just run and run and run. Who would have thought she could have kept that knife so well hidden in the waistband of that black plastic crap skirt for so long?

His wife was watching the late BCTV news when he came home after his shift.

"Terrible," she said. "That poor little girl. What was that mother doing?"

He had no clue what she was talking about and went into the apartment kitchen and put his lunch kit on the counter and poured the coffee she made for him because he would not be able to sleep until two thirty anyway. He never could when he was driving the three to ten-thirty shift.

He went into the bedroom and hung up his bus driver's uniform jacket and put his shirt into the laundry hamper and sat down on the side of the bed to take off his shoes and socks. He flexed his feet to relieve the cramps of a full shift pushing pedals. Passengers had no idea how hard driving a bus was on the driver's feet.

His wife had made the bed, which was a good sign even if she didn't say hello to him when he came in the door. He returned to the living room wearing his undershirt and driver's pants and sat in the chair they had brought home from their daughter's apartment a few weeks after they got the last call about her. He sipped his coffee and waited for the news to end and the sports to come on.

One of the many things he resented about still not having enough seniority to work straight days was missing Monday Night Football, though less now with Howard Cosell gone. People hated Cosell for being a loud-mouthed Jew who used big words, but at least he spoke well, had an orderly mind and was a good reporter. The new guy, O.J. Simpson, might have been an exciting running back, but off the field and in the Monday Night broadcast booth, he was not the sharpest knife in the drawer.

"Leaving her child alone in the house with a vicious dog," his wife said. "I can't believe a mother would do that. She should be thrown in jail."

"You won't believe," he said, "what happened on the route tonight."

"How would you know what I would believe," she said, "until you tell me?"

"A woman," he said, "doing you-know-what to herself. Right in a front seat. Doing you-know-what in public."

"What?" his wife said.

He put his coffee mug down on the living-room table. He looked at her and made a gesture with his fingers. She looked at him and when he saw she got it, he dropped his arm down beside the arm of the chair.

"What," she said, "a disgusting thing to say."

"The worst part," he said, "was some guy – some creep with a big beard – sitting there egging her on. Sitting across from her getting his jollies. And the cop gives me shit. Heck."

"Language," his wife said.

"I said 'heck.'"

"You used the s-word first. What cop?"

The sportscast came on, so he didn't have to answer her. The NFL highlight reel showed New York Giants' outside linebacker

Lawrence Taylor sacking Redskins' quarterback Joe Theisman. There was Theisman stepping up into the pocket to throw and here came Taylor looping in from the outside, driving full speed and launching himself with both arms above his helmet, generating so much force that he looked like a man leaping off a cliff and, instead of falling, defying gravity to rise up, up, up toward a mountain peak. Then gravity won its own back and Taylor crashed down on the quarterback's back, crumpling the quarterback into the turf with such ferocity that Theisman's planted leg collapsed in two directions at once, snapping his shin bone so it stuck up in the air with a bone point visible at a 45-degree angle while his foot was pressed flat against the ground as if someone had left a set of discarded toes on the field.

"What cop?" his wife said.

Now he could not have answered her if he'd wanted to. Part of him felt as if he'd just watched his own leg being snapped in two. Part of him was flapping to find the remote to turn the TV off in case they showed the clip again.

"Jesus," he said, "Christ."

"What," his wife said, "kind of language is that in this house?"

Yet he could not look away as Taylor leaped again into the air above Theisman's body, pounding his hands on the sides of his Giants' blue helmet. At first, the leaping and pounding seemed part of some savage victory dance. Then it became obvious Taylor was in agony of his own, screaming at the sidelines for someone to come and help. The arms that moments earlier were powering him upwards now flailed the uncomprehending air as he screamed and screamed for help that, in the highlight clip, never came.

"What," his wife said, "are you shouting about? You'll have a heart attack."

He hit the right button. The TV screen went black. Pain, physical agony, subsided from his forehead, down his neck, through his chest, along his thighs, out the bottoms of his feet.

"What," his wife said, "was that all about?"

She had seen nothing or, if she had seen it, had not understood what he'd just watched. How was it possible to explain a thing like that to her?

"I saw him," he said.

"Who?" his wife said. "Jesus?"

He listened to her. When she stayed home all day, she sometimes went back to sneaking the drinks, and when she snuck the drinks she became obtuse and tried to cover it with mockery, funny or cruel, that she could no more control than she could control the slurring of her words. Jesus would bring out the slurring if there was any for him to hear.

"No," he said, "Joe Theisman. He played in the CFL before he went to the NFL. He was in the Grey Cup in '71 or '72, I can't remember. My uncle got us tickets. I sat in Empire Stadium and watched him play quarterback for the Toronto Argonauts."

"I haven't got a clue," his wife said, "what you are talking about."

"Forget it," he said. "It was nothing."

"You said the cops were involved," his wife said. "It was something if the cops were involved."

She was right. It was something. They took the bag lady away in an ambulance. The big lump with the red beard wasn't hurt, but he looked shaken up.

"They weren't involved with me," he said. "I called them. I stopped the bus and threw them off."

"Threw who off?" his wife said.

He picked up his coffee cup and sat back in his daughter's chair. When she was little, they had a chair somewhat like it and she would curl up beside him and he would read to her from *Horton Hears a Who*.

"The woman," he said, "who was doing you-know-what to

herself. And the creep egging her on. I called the cops. The cop shows up and yells at me. Like I was the one in the wrong."

"People are becoming," his wife said, "animals."

"All I did," he said, "was stop the bus. I wasn't having that on my bus. I wasn't in the wrong."

"What is happening," his wife said, "to our world?"

As if getting up out of old habit to get her an answer, he took his coffee cup into the kitchen and pulled a knife out of the utensil drawer and made himself a thick peanut butter sandwich. He walked over and opened the white cotton curtains to look out the kitchen window. It was a Vancouver night when the yellow and silver lights of the downtown office towers and the blue-black wall of the North Shore Mountains, The Lions watching over them, were wrapped in mist the colour of smoke.

He called his wife to come and look with him, but she had turned the TV back on and stayed on the couch. It didn't matter. He ate his sandwich. Tomorrow, rain or shine, was another day.

PETER STOCKLAND is a native of British Columbia. He lives in Montreal but considers Calgary and Rome his true homes.